WITHIN Sunshine & SHADOW

THREE SHORT STORIES AND A NOVELLA

ALINA LONECK

I dedicate this collection to the ties that connect us all as we journey through life to discover who we are and who we are not.

In life you find three kinds of people: those who will change your life, those who will harm your life and those who will be your life.

Anonymous

The eye is always caught by light, but shadows have more to say.

Gregory Maguire

Contents

Introduction

Why the title, *Within Sunshine and Shadow*?

The themes of this short story collection come from the sunlit side of life as well as the shadowed: without one, there is not the other. Sometimes life is sunburst moments but, for the most part, we are continually traversing light and shadow as we deal with relationships and situations. While light imbues us with joy and contentment, shadows invite us to reflect, lick our wounds and, hopefully, fulfil the innate purpose of all living things – growth.

Within Sunshine and Shadows opens with three stories at the short's sweet spot and concludes with a novella.

Each story is compelling, insightful, highly nuanced and told with psychological precision. All are willing to explore the depths and hard truths of what it is to be human.

The Wrong Man

Relationships end for a single reason. Infidelity. Abuse. Incompatibility. No explanation needed. But sometimes, a reason requires a story. This is such a story.

SUMMER

Samantha Bonner believes in making her own sunshine, preferably shaken and stirred by a warm breeze and saltwater. She dives into the limpid ocean and, as her body glides across its infinite crispness, she notices the surface undulations diamond-studded in the sunlight and the sandy-slivered fingerlings that dart beneath and across her path. This is Heaven on Earth. Exiting the water she lets out a soft, "Oooh, so nice." She suns herself dry. Lying there, the need she's felt for months rises in her breast subtle and instinctual – longing and desire. She doesn't want her bare imprints on the tideline's wet sand to be forever those of a solitary in thought. She wants footprints of paired chatter: size elevens alongside her sixes. Her right hand stirs the depths of her beach bag. Found it. Her index finger taps the phone icon on her iPhone.

"Hello, my darling friend, guess what?"

"Hi, Sami, you sound excited. I'm taking a punt that whatever the guess what is, it's good news."

"I've decided to do what you've been telling me to do for ages. I'm going online to look for a good man to share my retirement with."

"That's fantastic. I'm so pleased. You've got a lot to offer. You're attractive, smart, loving and loyal, with the patience and wisdom of a saint."

"Thanks, Jenna … ooh, hang on a minute … I think I've just developed swelling on the brain, and my halo needs an upgrade."

"Ha-ha. You're a hoot."

"I'm thinking about RSVP. Madeline's niece is married to a great guy she met on there. Her family adores him … mind you … Madeline didn't do so well."

"Look, sweetheart, it's a mixed bag out there. You'll be fine. Keep me posted."

"Will do. I love you. Bye."

"I love you too. Good luck."

That evening Samantha logs into RSVP and, confident Van Morrison won't mind, decides on 'Tupelo Honey' as her profile name. She types: *My photos are from this year and untouched by the edit button; although, at my stage in life, I present better by candlelight and minus prescription glasses.* Why do most men think women lie about their age? She'd never do that. Tell one lie and all your truth becomes questionable. Next question. What are you looking for in a man? She wants to avoid it sounding like a shopping list, but she knows what she appreciates: kindness, intelligence, wit, humour and fidelity. What's important to her in a partner is a man with a stable, robust sense of self, connected to others and contributing positively to their lives.

Account activated. *Phew!*

During the first three weeks, her RSVP inbox is a steady stream of notifications. Online texts, phone calls and then coffee – rounds of one or two-way eliminations. Third up is Martin. He drives an hour and a half to meet her at Anchor's Wharf Restaurant for lunch. *Three brownie points.* He's well educated, and the conversation flows. *Two brownie points.* Sometimes his questions are too probing – *minus two.* He insists on paying for lunch. *Plus two.* It's a relief he's not a there's a moth-in-my-wallet sort of a guy. You know, the ones who ensure they don't pay the extra fifty cents because 'hers was the soy cappuccino'. She's met a few of those. When she and Martin leave, he opens the door for her, and then asks, "Well, would you like to catch up again?"

"That would be great. We'll chat during the week." She goes to hug him. He kisses her full on the lips – *minus five.*

A stream of unsuitable others follow on from Martin, including those who have played the online game too long and can't be bothered to make any effort. "I'll be passing through Grafton on the way to a fishing trip. I could meet you at McDonald's for a coffee."

Seriously? Seventy-nine kilometres for a substandard coffee?

After the first three weeks, the messages slow to a trickle. Samantha's fended off the odd-bods, the twenty-five-year-olds and the over-sharers. *Really*, does she need to know the reason a man stayed with his alcoholic wife was that she was intelligent and the sex was fantastic?

Samantha is over it all by the time she agrees to a walk on the beach with Mark Hollerman – Karm47. She's impressed by his inventive letter-play. He appears charming, attentive, authentic, well-travelled and intelligent, *and* he drives for Meals on Wheels twice a week. His teeth distract her; they look as if they've been laid by a tiler. Hollywood has a lot to answer for. She thinks of her overbite; at least her teeth are naturally straight. She shares her travel to-dos. "I'd love to visit Japan and then, from Vladivostok, take the Trans-Siberian into Russia and finish in Poland."

"That's amazing. All those places are on my list too."

Mark's response surprises Samantha: raised eyebrows, open mouth and upward-facing palms. He must *really* want to do that. When their walk comes to an end, he asks, "Would you like to see a show next week at the club? I'll pick up the tickets."

"I love live shows. That'd be wonderful, Mark. Thank you."

The night of the concert, Mark picks her up. Samantha opens the door in a black off-the-shoulder, below-the-knee, sheath dress with three-quarter sleeves. She's accessorised entirely in white. "Wow!" is all he says, but she sees the hallelujah in his eyes, hears it in the tone of his voice. She glances at his navy tailored jacket paired with café au lait trousers and spit-and-polish Oxfords. Clothes always look good on tall, lean men. "You look so debonair. We both brush up rather well, don't we?"

At the end of the evening, when he says goodnight on her porch, he cups her hands in his. "You must have sensed how hard it was for me to keep my eyes and hands off you. Your long neck. Those beautiful shoulders."

"Perhaps," she says, but really she had no idea. He kisses her on the cheek, and she relaxes into knowing Mark is a gentleman and that she wants to explore a relationship with him.

So much they do together is a perfect fit. Cooking together, Mark and Samantha's tempos are in unison; he finishes chopping just as she's ready to cook. At rock'n'roll lessons his lead is firm but gentle. Apart from one another their texts are frequent, flirty and loving and their phone calls long.

Two months into the relationship, he arrives at her house and greets her with, "You know, I was listening to a podcast and this writer ... I can't remember her name ... was saying that the best way to describe herself was that she was a sponge always soaking up ideas, and I thought, *that's you*. Now I understand why, when we go anywhere, you read every informative plaque and google every passing fancy. You *really* are so *delightfully* and *uniquely* you."

Oh my god! Mark sees her, he understands her, he knows who she is. "This is the first time in a relationship I've felt truly seen for who I am."

He holds her close.

He feels like home to her.

AUTUMN

Mark potters in the garden the mornings he sleeps over. Hearing him whistle among the greenery makes Samantha's entire body Frangelico-infused. Is she in love? Not yet. Smitten. That's the word she'd use.

One morning, three months into the relationship, there's an, "I love you, Sami. It'd be great if we lived together." She's taken aback. Partnership, home and belonging. She gets it. He has none of the three. It must be unsettling at seventy to be living in a caravan no matter how well set up it is. "Mark, it's wonderful to hear those words, but I can't reciprocate. It's just too early for me. I so enjoy being with you, but we still don't fully know one another. You haven't seen me stressed, irritable or revoltingly sick. Could we take a step back for the moment?"

Days later, there's an, "I adore you, Samantha."

"What do you adore about me, Mark?" He's silent. There's a nonplussed look on his face as if he's been asked a question he can't answer.

In the weeks that follow, Samantha notices other incongruent behaviours she struggles to understand. He's taking over in the garden. One morning she pops out for his favourite newspaper, *The Weekend Australian*, and returns to find he's removed a small, glossy-leafed tree she rather liked. "It had to go. It blocked the view of the pond from the patio." She wishes he'd checked all angles. The bedroom is now without privacy.

The pruning continues the weekends he stays over. He confiscates shrubs and small trees without consultation.

Samantha tries to get her point across light-heartedly with a hug and a smile. Smiles always reassure him. "Mark, I truly appreciate all you do in the garden. I love the lumberjack in you, but the garden's becoming a *Where's that shrub gone?* Thank goodness neither of us owns a chainsaw. Remind me to keep you well away from aisle twenty-two at Bunnings." He stares at her and says nothing. The two-way channel's on mute. She's become a soliloquy mired in sludge. He returns to the garden and downscales the pruning to excess offshoots from the golden palms. Samantha smiles to herself – boys and sticks, men and lumber.

A few weeks later, there's another garden incident. Samantha does not want to look out on piles of garden waste and worries about vermin and snakes. She begins to remove one of them.

"*Leave it!*"

It spits out from between his lips like charcoaled bread from a toaster. It's a stalemate. She removes the piles when he's not there. Of course, he'll notice. He'll say nothing.

As autumn increasingly loses heat, and leaves rust and fall away, the air between Samantha and Mark becomes laden with the covert – his withdrawal, his withholding, his stonewalling. Everything in the garden is *not* fine.

Marina Prior and David Hobson are on tour with their *The 2 of Us* show and are appearing at the local RSL. Samantha's keen to see them. "I think we should go. They're both legends of opera and musical theatre: *Les Misérables*, *West Side Story*, *La Bohème*."

He is non-committal, so Samantha arranges tickets with her I-love-a-live-show girlfriend Michelle. A girls' night out.

A few days later at Tuesday night's rock'n'roll class at the RSL, Samantha nips to the loo before they head home. She meets him in the foyer, but it's not till they are at home he tells her he has bought a ticket to the show. She's astounded, but then again, he does have a habit of uncommunicated three-sixties.

"I wonder if your seat is anywhere near us, Mark?" She unpins the tickets for Michelle and herself from the memo board in her walk-in pantry. "Fifty-eight and fifty-nine."

He's incredulous. "Mine's sixty. What are the chances of that, Samantha? Same table and a seat near yours. What a coincidence."

"*Wow!* Unbelievable."

Something deliberate, slow and precise is playing out. So imperceptible at first, Samantha becomes a player in it, but the script and the part she plays are withheld from her. He's sucking the vitality out of her with his constant need for validation and compliance. Weekends together – cottonwool and eggshells. She's becoming someone she struggles to recognise, a lit candle in a draughty corner. She doesn't understand why, after six months, after she's fallen in love with him, sex has become as infrequent as their shared outdoor activities. It's as if Mark is going through the motions, as if acting a part is catching up with him. She's beginning to see he uses sex and certain behaviours to control her when he feels insecure. What was once cute banter morphs into the monotone violence of barbs. Samantha no longer feels safe, seen, heard or held. Forgetful now of the small things, one morning she asks him, "What time do we go to singing tonight?"

"What time do you think we usually go?"

"I'm not sure, that's why I'm asking you."

A raised eyebrow, an impatient breath. "You know you don't remember things that clearly. You probably don't even know what the date is today."

His response unsettles her.

Myriad indirect hints about moving in lurk, but Samantha is not accepting responsibility for housing him. It is his problem to solve, not hers.

"My son wants to borrow the Kedron Top Ender in April to show his American girlfriend around Australia."

"Where will you live if you agree to that?"

"It's going to be cold in the caravan over winter."

Samantha ignores the statement.

"It's damn difficult keeping track of things when they're in three places: my caravan, the storage shed and your house."

"Mark, you really should rent somewhere of your own. We've talked about this before. It would make things so much easier for you." It would also prove something of paramount importance to her – is Mark with her solely because of her home? She knows he won't rent. Since the concert, his wallet has been a thin sandwich in want of her filling. She's been more than fair. Five months after meeting him, she had to stay in Sydney for a week for eye surgery. She was relieved he was happy to come with her and drive her back in her car. Samantha made it clear she'd pay for petrol, accommodation and any associated costs. It dismayed her that the only time he reached into his wallet was for a serving of fish and chips at the beach on the last day. It was worse than the time he'd bought an eight-dollar sandwich to share and asked her for half the cost, especially after all those three-course meals she'd cooked him.

Meanness, so unattractive.

Still, there are worse things a man can be.

One afternoon the week before their planned trip to Vietnam, out of the blue comes, "I don't think being faithful is that important. My mother and father had affairs. They stayed together and became closer as they got older."

What! They'd discussed the importance of monogamy from the beginning. Had Mark forgotten her profile? What had happened to his mantra, 'Trust and Be True'? It's shifting sand too far. She knows the dangers of quicksand sand, she's read *The Worst-Case Scenario Survival Handbook* and noted its sub-title *Great Escapes and Entrances*: toss what's weighing you down; take a step or two backwards; pull yourself out with whatever is at hand. If all fails, float. She takes a deep breath, then slowly and deliberately says, "Mark, it's over." He takes a step back, sucks in his breath, says nothing and leaves. When the front door closes, Samantha lets the air escape deep from within her lungs, long and slow. It's a breath she's held for far too long.

What to do? Return flights for two have been booked and paid for but not the hotels. Damn it, she's going anyway. Mark can do what he sees fit. He pulls out. For the first time in eight months she feels she can breathe.

At midnight the day before departure, her phone pings with a text message alert.

I've decided to go. I've booked a hotel in Hanoi for sixteen days.

What! He hates cities; there's a whole country to see. She texts back.

You must be mad or drunk.

She understands Mark deciding to go but, Hanoi, for sixteen days? This man has no sense of who he is. His responses are either set in stone or cartwheel and flutter adrift on an anxious, shifting breeze.

There's a text from him the morning of their late afternoon departure.

Can I get a lift with you to the airport?

She's not sure if he's still wanting things from her or is just too mean to pay for a taxi. Probably both. Samantha doesn't want to be petty. She responds with, *OK.*

Sitting next to him on the plane, she's surprised by her composure. Whatever they had is in the past now. She's never been a waverer; she is travelling alone when she's there. A song from the musical *South Pacific* starts up in her head. 'I'm gonna wash that man right outa my hair and send him on his way. Yea, sister!' Oh, that's comforting – like a pacifier to a baby.

"You can stay at my hotel in Hanoi if you like," he says casually. "It's a double room."

"No need. I've booked a room in the InterContinental Westlake."

During the three weeks, she travels solo happily and enjoys the pure luxury of hotels with pools – a blissful swim before breakfast and at the end of the day. In Hoi An she hires a local moto driver, Chum, and explores with the sun on her skin, the wind in her hair. She is fulfilled. She is free. She ignores Mark's texts – his problems are no longer hers.

On the one a.m. return flight he has the window seat. He lifts his right arm. "Come here, rest against me, it'll be easier to sleep."

"Are you sure? You look very cramped."

"I'm fine. Really."

She leans back against his chest, her head on his shoulder. He strokes her hair tenderly. She is not fully aware it is all a deliberate technique to lure her back.

They reunite on their return.

WINTER

Samantha refuses to respond to Mark's continuing hints about moving in. Sensing his mounting frustration, she's surprised when he suggests a fossicking trip to Tingha in the Kedron Top Ender. The caravan is like the playhouse she had when she was a child – intimate and compactly perfect.

On the way they stop overnight at Native Dog Campground in Cathedral Rock National Park, Ebor. The star-luminous sky is clear and moonless as the crackle and blaze of a massive log fire warms their fronts as their backs chill in equal measure. Mark connects the BOSE to his iPhone playlist, and opera overwhelms the icy darkness. Struck by the beauty of it, Samantha cries. He looks at her with moist eyes and cradles her.

This trip however, is when Mark Hollerman shape-shifts to Mark Pettiman. Mark Pettiman, the man who deliberately and unintentionally didn't fill up the water tank in the Kedron before they left. The man who stores plastic buckets and caravan paraphernalia in the shower forcing Samantha to say, "I need to have a quick shower. You know I'm in there for under ten seconds. I need to freshen up down under." She feels a little humiliated having to spell out her hygiene needs. He hides the hot water bottle under the bed so she can't use it. He buys two-dollar white bread knowing she only eats sourdough. She challenges him, he relents. It becomes the pattern of the trip.

The day before heading back home from Tingha, Mark decides to do some sunrise fossicking. "I'll be back for lunch." At midday, Samantha begins to prepare lunch. One o'clock … two o'clock … no show. Mark has the car, the caravan park no bikes, and she hurt her toe when she walked barefoot into a wall at home in the dark the day before they left. She's stranded with no good book to read. By late afternoon, she gingerly makes her way to the town's cemetery. There, she uprights what yesterday's wind blew over and scattered, and she leaves the cemetery feeling less like a stranger in this township of boulders. Mark returns at dusk – no explanation, no apologies. He doesn't want her to help him with the dinner. He sleeps with his back to her. They're a pair of strangers in tinned cold storage.

Progressively and inwardly, Samantha becomes the husk of a cicada shedding, her inner happiness and confidence browned and brittle – her lover is now her adversary. Time is consumed managing his feelings and unspoken demands, leaving no time to build a relationship. Her body's adrenals pump cortisol and inflammatory chemicals; long gone are the days of dopamine and serotonin as chi drains from her like a tap in need of a washer. Mark's dissonance has done this to her, and she, she has allowed it in the belief that relationships take work but suspecting it shouldn't be this hard.

The evening of the fundraiser for ovarian cancer is the night Mark Hollerman reveals the second man lurking inside him – Phil Anderer – when he makes a deliberate choice to sit apart from Samantha to send a message to the woman across from them of his sexual interest. Samantha is hurt and incensed by his eyebrow-flashing and man-on-offer crotch display.

What's evident to Samantha is apparent to the others close by who glance over, look away, mutter and nod among themselves; he needs to revive himself with another woman with sleek dark hair, a kitten-nose, anaphylactic lips and breasts that would be more at home on a soccer field.

His two-way conversation is all chilli and hot chocolate, *we* and *us* inconsequential and forgotten. *How dare he behave like this*! Worse is coming. Samantha's jaw tightens vice-like, and hot ice rises in her chest. She's distracted for a moment, as a friend taps her on the shoulder to say goodbye. As Samantha turns her back, she hears the faint but characteristic click of a retractable pen, glimpses a beer mat deposited into a handbag, witnesses Phil Anderer's right hand slide out across the left side of his chest between jacket lapel and shirt. It's the crossing of the line – the line between sexual attraction and intentional infidelity.

When Mark and Samantha leave, twilight has turned to dank dusk. They walk the fifteen minutes home in severed silence. He hasn't proffered his hand for her to take as he usually would. He isn't walking kerbside either. She hunches her shoulders and tucks her hands under her armpits against the callous chill of the night, her head a hot confusion of thoughts, her heart stuck on pause. She knows when they reach home there will be a third aberration. He will walk through the door ahead of her and, when he does, she knows what she must do: hold onto her values, be true to who she is and abandon what places her at risk of compromising both.

Mark takes off his shoes, plonks down on the lounge in the media room and reaches for the remote. Samantha tentatively follows him in. The timing's not right for an 'I-need-to-talk-to-you' conversation, but she's now a car with its brake-line cut. "There's something I need to ask you."

He looks at her like she's a piece of grit in his shoe. He says nothing.

She sits down on the couch as far away from him as possible, asks a matter-of-fact question in need of the staccato simplicity of a yes or no. She is attentive to timing and clusters that will tell her one thing she needs to know – will he lie to her? Within the first five seconds, she asks him three times, "Did you arrange to catch up with that woman?"

The living room swallows the silence; it settles in the corners numb and skeletal. He's a marble statue on display whose blank eyes pin Samantha like an overturned truck. The prolonged eye contact tells her one thing. He is not a deer in the headlights, he's a compulsive liar put on the spot. *Failure to answer – liar.*

Behind his frozen façade his mind is thinking at a thousand words a minute; he is buying time to decide how to respond. He cannot admit a 'yes' because everything will crumble within him and around him. Samantha's learnt that shame for him is nothing more than the discomfort of being unmasked. She asks a fourth time, "Well, did you?" She waits for the first trickle and the stream of deviations that will follow.

"People chat. Some – people – happen – to – be – women."

Does he think she's stupid? *Failure to deny – liar, liar.*

She is silent. She knows what she saw. She now, knows Mark.

He rises from the lounge and, like a hyena about to scavenge on leftovers, circles around to the right of her. Samantha waits … still no yes or no. Shock? Hurt? Indignance? There is none of that.

"You're so damn distrusting and insecure. Have you been burnt before?"

Enough already! She has known for some time the nine words necessary to sever the relationship. Out they spill. "I've decided I don't want to live with you."

All he asks is, "You mean you never want to live with anyone or just not with me?"

She is in no mood to be generous, to share any more of herself with him or let any of her energy flow into him. Armoured, she is calm and forthright. "It's a decision I'm making at this moment in time and, at this moment in time, you are the person I'm making it about." It's so icily perfect. She's stunned and appalled when he asks if he can take home some of the dessert she made, and promised him, the previous night. She wishes she was the sort of woman that would tell him to *fuck off.*

Within the week he comes twice to remove his belongings stored in the garage. He'll have to go back to paying a hundred and twenty-five dollars a month for a storage shed. When he returns for the last time, Samantha has already filled the empty spaces left by the absence of his belongings.

"You've wasted no time in rearranging things." There is no hurt in his voice, only accusation.

"I did that because I couldn't bear to look at the empty spaces." He says nothing.

Samantha knows he does not believe her words. He can't trust her truth because he can't trust his own. She avoids looking at him. Finished, he stands in the driveway with the detached amusement of someone who is playing a game. A burning sensation rises into her chest and throat, souring her mouth. Ashamed she ever loved *this* man, she turns her back and presses the garage door controller on the wall.

The roller door wheezes and clanks until it hits concrete.

SPRING

Extricated, Samantha's left with a toxic residue. A black, sticky soot clings to her psyche. She rebukes herself with *I ought to have, I should have;* yet, she was so close to mental collapse she struggled to think clearly. What most does her head in is trying to determine what was real and what from the outset was a crafted illusion. It takes Samantha a month to realise she's unable to process and heal the damage the relationship has caused. She needs professional help.

Samantha is grateful that the Women's Resource Centre will see her immediately.

The counsellor Emily understands the dynamic completely: borderline personality disorder. He's a narcissistic waif. "These types of men are involved in domestic violence: emotional, physical, psychological. They look for women who are empathetic, generous, compassionate, tolerant, loyal and forgiving. They also look for a strong woman but resent her strength. Strength is a threat."

"I'm a wise, intelligent woman. Why did I not figure this out sooner?"

"Think of these people as a black hole, a parasite, a vampire, an abyss that can't be filled. They're masters at sourcing a supply of energy, adoration and, in some cases, money. Take away their supply and they have nothing to offer. I had a client recently who'd been married to one for forty years. Only now is she realising what she was dealing with all those years."

"Really … poor woman. I know I felt like I was going crazy."

"Women trapped in relationships like this often suffer from deep depression caused by years of criticism and contempt. When the abusive spouse dies, the partner is conflicted between grief and relief."

"What makes those with BDP like that?"

"People with borderline personality disorder have problems relating to themselves and others. They don't know who they are, which is why their behaviour is so inconsistent. They lie and can't admit mistakes because they already feel less-than. They avoid feeling shame at all costs."

"Will he do this to someone else?"

"Absolutely. Your ex will feel no remorse and have no desire to change. BPD's often suffer from anxiety due to a deep sense of emptiness and isolation. That's why, even when it's over, they hover even though the woman's made it clear she wants no contact."

"*Oh my god*, that's what he did with me. I made it very clear it was over. No contact. But he just kept on going – a blaming, petty letter in my mailbox, texts, emails. I blocked him. Relentless, he'd pop up in my mailbox with *yet another* email address. I felt like a mouse being toyed with by a cat. I called the police, and they rang him. Apart from one last text – *May your god forgive you* – he's left me alone."

"Are either of you religious?"

"No … just a barb to make me feel bad about myself."

"Calling the police was a smart move. As you discovered, once outed, they stop hovering. Otherwise, it's another week, another month, another year."

The session time is up.

"Thank you so much, Emily, for tiding me over till my first appointment with the psychologist. I was desperate to have my experience validated. Most of my friends simply didn't understand. I'd share things, and they'd look at me strangely as if I was making it up or exaggerating. Only one of my closest friends, Jenna, understood because her ex-husband was cruel and controlling."

With the relationship behind her, everything is see-through to Samantha: what confused her, what she didn't see. She begins to see the bitter demise of Mark's marriage in another light and why his ex-wife hired a top solicitor and told their only son (who was thirty-two at the time) never to mention his name again in her presence. Samantha understands why, after a long, stressful marriage and at least two affairs – well, the two he had chosen to share with her – his wife blamed him for her ovarian cancer. At the time Samantha spouted something from a podcast – men have affairs to stay in a marriage, women to leave it. She can see him now. How her words lapped gently over him, suffusing his eyes with a preferred reality; the persona non grata now believed he was the long-suffering, worthy hero. His response to her tears in Ebor? She was just a mirror in which he saw himself reflected. Her confusion over his behaviour on the Tingha trip? He resented her being in his home. Everything made sense. *What an idiot she'd been.*

After eight monthly sessions with the psychologist, Samantha is a woman laundered.

She's regained much of who she is but, beneath the surface, she knows she will never be the same – something lost, some-thing gained. She'd valued him, loved him, and that was her undoing. He'd lured her with her wounding: to love and to be fully seen and loved in return. Eventually, she had challenged his truth, and he'd shrivelled like thin plastic before a flame.

Samantha Bonner is sure of one thing – she will never, never, never kiss beneath a parasitic plant again. With her newfound awareness, she lets go of one female friend of a few months with similar traits. In quick succession, life tests her with Lionel and Robert, newcomers to her informal social circle. She susses Lionel out in a few weeks: an attention-seeking, immature wuss. Gone. Robert? She doesn't even go there.

What she is not sure of is how deeply the collateral damage has wounded her. Currently, the red hand on her compass is facing towards the safety of the solo and the celibate. Samantha's no feminist, but perhaps Gloria Steinem was right: *A woman without a man is like a fish without a bicycle.* But then again, summer is just around the corner.

Losing Una

As the prison gate closed behind him, he saw someone he recognised.
I knew she only gave in because she was lonely. Only child.
Single. Motherless and the wrong side of forty. I recognised
her as you do someone with whom you are familiar. You sense
it, know by sight their walk, their posture. Seconds before
the gate closed, I turned. As I turned, I caught the moment.
The moment her stiff stillness became the staccato click-clack
of heels on the concrete fading to snow-cold silence. The
moment her black-and-white judgement won out over the
redemptive synergy of forgiveness and memory.

I had drained her mother of colour – a pillow against her face. A face that no longer recognised those she loved. A mind that could not hold onto the present, the past a loop of successive takes. There was no rain that night and, above the stilled silence, a full moon. I blurted out on the phone, "Your mother is dead." Numb muteness, and then her tears as I stonewalled my heart in silent, static misery and longed for the unrecoverable.

For my act of loving violence, at sixty-four, I am lost to the world for ten years – perhaps to my daughter forever. I must wait and hope. Trust that she will forgive me for having loved so deeply and always said, and shown, too little.

Amongst her mother's possessions she found …
I am angry. Alone. I cry myself to sleep. *All this because of you!* I hate myself for missing you when all I want is the freedom of indifference. I hate you for leaving me to sort out my mother's possessions, forcing me to remember what I try so hard to forget. *Hate you. Hate you.* Hate you for the problem of the box to which *you* have the key.

A writing lap travel box of flame mahogany, inlaid brassware and joints dovetailed to patient perfection. You made it for Mother for an anniversary, and we gave it to her together over breakfast. I was six at the time. In the night I was woken by soft music and, as I reached the bottom of the stairs, there you were dancing with my mother. As a child, I felt safe and loved when your large hands lifted and hugged me, but that night I noticed something else as your hands held the small of Mother's back and her silky shoulder, something beyond a child's understanding. I understand it now – intimacy and tenderness.

I stare at the box. It beckons, *open me … you know you must.* It's the must I walked away from yesterday. *You* have the key. I need to know what is inside.

Reluctantly he handed over the key.
Lockets. Diaries. Letters. These are private affairs, and I am a very private man. The request for the key is typewritten. It arrives the day after my daughter chose to turn around and walk away. The signature is Times New Roman, twelve-point as if ink, like blood, is too personal a marker. I relent. What she will find can only do good where I appear to have harmed.

Since I requested the key, I'm still sorting through my mother's things. I pause for a break and look out of the bedroom window. It's early afternoon. A dull day uncertain whether it is sun or cloud. The doubtful sky reveals slices of sunlight as it peek-a-boos with the clouds.

The doorbell rings. I rush from the back of the house to the front and unlock the door, but no one's there. I look downward, and propped against the terracotta plant pot is a small Express Post padded bag. I know what's inside. I'll open it tomorrow.

After breakfast the next day, I open the box expecting to find a diary, papers and a bundle of letters. Instead, I discover only three things.

The first sits atop an envelope as if freshly taken off. It's my mother's large Victorian black enamel locket and 18ct gold belcher chain. Inlaid gold swirls of delicate, trailing stems and leaves edge the heart. In the centre, a $\mathcal{U}$ – Una. She wore the locket always. It encircled her slender neck just short of the valley between her breasts. I slip it off the chain, place it in the palm of my right hand and roof my fingers over it enclosing it like a precious pearl inside an oyster shell. I close my eyes. Slowly, the heat of my hand warms the enamel. I see my mother's svelte body, delicate features and bobbed, straight, black hair and hazel eyes. Never vanilla, she was an emerald green and buttercup-yellow woman with a magical ability to draw others to her.

I open my hand and then the locket. On the left, my father as a young man looks out at me: blonde hair that dips into a widow's peak and deep-set, heavy-lidded brown eyes, high cheekbones and full lips. My father's default face, pensive, became joyous when he smiled and laughed. His calm depths allowed my mother's melody to glisten. Others were drawn to him because his quiet assuredness aroused curiosity. Everyone listened when he spoke. On the right, I see me as a girl, pensive and unsmiling. *How I hated being photographed.* I have my mother's hair and my father's eyes. I close the locket, place it back in the box and pick up the envelope. I recognise its bespoke white linen paper and its red silk lining. My father's paper of choice.

14th February 1980

Happy anniversary, my darling!

I knew when I first saw you, that you were the one for me.

We have been married ten years and still, every time I put my arms around you, I feel that I am home. I know you experience the same because when my hands stroke your back and you nuzzle into me, you shiver, and I see the goosebumps rise on your bare arms.

Such tenderness I feel for you and a passion hidden from everyone but us. I am yours forever, my darling friend, companion and lover.

We both know life can be unpredictable and fragile. Please remember, in sickness and in health, you will always be precious to me. At such times, I will be your rock. There is nothing I will not do to protect you and our darling daughter.

Your adoring husband,

Peter. xx

How he cherished her. How at times I felt overlooked. An outsider. A welcome visitor in a home marked by two. My father, our protector. Is this what this is all about? Is his mute acceptance of the prison sentence penance for what he did? Is it about exiling himself from a life that has no meaning beyond her? Am I so angry because he felt I needed shielding from the progression of my mother's disease? I have no answers.

The final item is a beige fabric pouch like an oversized spectacle case. It has two pockets with zippers. I open the smaller, lower pocket to find it contains two AA batteries and an ear receiver. I open the top zipper, shake the pouch and out slides a silver Sony IC recorder the size of a chunky KitKat – the locked-away answers to my questions. My instinct tells me that whatever it contains, it's not going to be easy listening. I put everything back in the pouch and leave it on the coffee table for another day.

My night in bed is full of wakefulness and dreams, both invaded by an electrical current of fear that courses through my body, between my breasts and nibbles at my fingers. Relentless, it does not stop. Saturated with anxiety and exhaustion I surrender, and I am it. Still it refuses to leave.

When morning comes I lie in till eleven, my eyes masked against the sunlight. After a strong coffee and a light breakfast, I play the first message. It is fifteen minutes and fifty-six seconds long. My father has recorded it in high definition. I hear the piano – Beethoven's 'Moonlight Sonata'.

The first movement enraptures with its slow, steady, quiet tempo and sombre, rolling triplets that sway back and forth. The fleeting melody's light glistens through the dark notes. I see my mother's right hand, and her pinkie finger cutting through the accompaniment.

The second movement, where the notes run up and down the keyboard, is too light and flowery for my taste. It is as Liszt said, 'the flower between two chasms'. It is the third and final movement – dark, roaring, fluid, powerful and passionate – that holds me captive and breathless with its intense, unbridled, intricate rhythms and speed.

Emotionally exhausted from listening, I pause the recorder. My eyes linger on the wall filled with framed memories of a family intact. Now, I see only the gaps of bare wall between the photos as missing pieces of a jigsaw puzzle that spite has swallowed. My mother, a songbird on the wing, who flew over the fields unminding of the barbed wire fences below became tangled in what life held beyond the melodies and beautiful harmonies.

I need to eat or rest. I stop the recording unit and lie down to listen to a guided meditation on my iPhone. I hear the instructions (breath through your belly, then your chest, your abdomen), and then I am out. I wake up three hours later. It's four p.m. I am morose and groggy, having heard nothing of the app but the beginning but knowing why I am angry with them and angry with myself. Thoughts turn and tumble like balls in a tombola.

My father and my mother did what they did without including me.

I supported my father from a distance, but I should have done more.

It always seemed what was between them had space for only two.

Ends always have beginnings.

In the beginning were the mild anomalies in my mother's behaviour: forgetting where she'd placed something for safe-keeping; names that were once fluent on her tongue stalled or forgotten for a moment; an inability to focus on a task without her mind and actions diverted onto another track; her recall of events and conversations shaky; the banana skin in the top loader instead of the bin, until their multitude became the aberration that is Alzheimer's.

I noticed on my last visit, before my overseas transfer, how she found it increasingly difficult to follow conversations. During dinner she'd listen intently, a blank expression behind her eyes. She was lost. When she ceased to follow, she would interject with an off-topic, much repeated, amusing anecdote from her past. I'd say, 'Mother, you've told us this before' but she'd continue regardless, determined to be included. My mother now the outsider and between my father and me, the unspoken but the known. I always knew to say a 'yes' if she offered me a cup of tea; otherwise, she'd continue to ask because her memory needed a visual cue.

I stay in my pyjamas all day. All I want to do is cocoon.

At eight p.m. I curl up with a hot water bottle pressed against my chest, not because it's cold, but because I need to feel it's comforting warmth. At two a.m. I'm awake. I make a hot chocolate and sip as I listen to another recording; I skip to one mid-way on the unit. It begins with my father's voice.

"You play so beautifully, you always do. I can listen to you for hours."

Then my mother, an aware moment. "Peter, darling, I feel afraid. I'm lost. Something's missing. My heart knows it, and it creeps up on me like a dread … How long do we have?"

"Before you forget again?"

"Yes."

"Yesterday it was for five minutes."

"Days like this I'd rather be ignorant of my forgetfulness. I am a prisoner tortured by my emotions of fear, dread and panic." Then, her voice urgent and anxious, "Please, please, when I cease to exist, help me go. I know I can trust you to know when the time is right. Promise me that, Peter. I don't want to be palliated."

"My poor darling, I promise. For now, together, we will live in the present moment. Come what may, you will always exist for me." My father's voice is potent, calm and reassuring. "Here, let me sit behind you. Lean back against me so I can circle my arms around you. Let me warm your hands in mine. Close your eyes, feel our breath in rhythm, listen to my voice. Say after me – I am safe. I am loved."

She echoes it three times. She's suddenly calmed, diverted. "I'm so hungry."

"Come on. It's time for lunch. You know how you love egg, mayo and lettuce sandwiches with the crusts cut off. Let's go out and see if those good-for-protein pets of ours have laid any eggs." I hear the patio door open and then my mother's voice, "But it's snowing!" I hear my father laugh. "Una, it does look like snow. But it's spring, and it's the blossom from the pear tree. Look, see the bees? I know, I'll collect the eggs, and you can pick some flowers."

"*Look at me, Peter.* I'm swimming in sunshine. I'm so happy. I'm going to hug you."

In the silence that follows is, until he has control of his words, the space before tears when the cheeks warm and pressure builds up in the back of the throat. My father's voice quavers, "I love you, Una."

"I love you too. We love each other very much … hold my hand. I don't want to get lost in the park."

"I'll make sure you get home safely. We have eggs and flowers to take home, remember."

Awareness. Oblivion. A faulty power switch of reappear and disappear and the shrivelling in-between the two. All of it here. *How dare it rest so lightly in the palm of my hand?*

When my mother plateaued and then, within months, faltered, fell and disappeared beneath the waters of Lethe (the underworld river of forgetfulness), I recall her Lilliputian tributes to the beauty and freedom of the outdoors. I never knew my mother owned so many little vases. Raw compassion rose in my chest, intermingled with fear. Always she was a woman of the flamboyant, the intoxicating. A woman of the lily, gardenia and her favourite, night-scented jessamine because its botanical name sounded like a title for a piano composition – Cestrum nocturnum.

Now, she was smaller, flatter – a wallflower.

"How long has she been doing this with all the vases?" I asked my father at the time.

"It's just started. It gives your mother pleasure to wander freely in the garden now she doesn't have the autonomy to leave the house on her own anymore. You know how much beauty and independence meant to her."

"And the incontinence pads?"

"You found one?"

"I wondered what the smell in the wardrobe was when I went to hang up her dress from the dry-cleaners. She'd popped one into the pocket of a jacket."

"Poor darling, she's embarrassed. She's always hiding them. I just find them and get rid of them."

I bring myself back to the present. My need is not for my memories but for those entombed in the unit, the truth of the middling years of my mother's disease. I start the recording again. My father is beginning to lose her.

"Who are you?"

"I'm your husband Peter. That's you and me and Kate on the DVD we're watching. Do you know who Kate is?"

My mother stalls, "I'm trying to remember … do I know her?"

"She's our daughter, Una."

"What's the matter with me?"

It's the core question throughout the recordings she asks regularly like a short repeated phrase in music.

To entertain my mother and to stop them degrading, my father digitised all the old film reels from the 1950s and the videotapes from the seventies. When my mother heard the transferred sound from the high-end Super 8 movie reels my father took in the mid-sixties, she'd squeal with delight, her hands clapping like an excited five-year-old. Other times they distressed her as did the mirrors. My father removed every mirror in the house after she began to slap her reflection repeatedly and ask, "What are you doing here?" Her unre-membering frightened and confronted her and, like a bully, taunted her with her shortcomings. At these times I mar-velled how creative my father was with a box of high-quality art prints. He kept the images simple. They looked at them together and made up a story. I was a part of it once. A part of the remarkable, the magical. He'd fan out a few of the A5 prints like playing cards from a deck. "Choose one for us, Una … It's Banksy's *Girl with Balloon*. She looks happy to me. What do you think, Una?"

"Of course she's happy. She adores the wind in her hair and on her skin."

"She must like red too," I add.

"Yes, red is a happy colour. The little girl let the balloon go because she's sending it on the wind so that everyone who sees it will feel happy."

My father strokes my mother's hands gently. "I agree with you, Una."

"Me too," I say. "Look, the girl's feet are together. That means she's letting the balloon go. We could send a balloon of our own in the air."

"Yes, yes … *now*. I want to send lots of balloons in all different colours."

"We'll all go for a walk, buy the balloons, and Kate and I will blow them up."

My mother never turned down an invitation to go out; it's the only now of the before.

The girl and her red balloon – all I can see is a story of loss without hope. Like my mother, the balloon floats away to lie in some foreign place, deflated and less-than.

Gradually I stopped visiting as frequently and, the truth is, I hoped I didn't need to visit. It was a two-hour drive each way. I used the fact she no longer recognised me to justify my absence. If she cannot remember me, then surely, I cannot be missed. I avoided the joy I felt those times she remembered my name when I walked through the door, and I avoided the tearing grief when, in my eagerness to catch her with a hug, she'd slipped beyond me, unable to reciprocate. That day, I left with a mantra in my head. Do not look back, walk away *as fast as you can*. Shame surges and quavers in my chest with the raw acknowledgement I not only thought this, I acted upon it.

I restart the recording. The middle folders are conversations between the two of them: halting, dreamy and repetitive minutiae of caring freighted with unspeakable pain. A vase becomes a cup, a comb a toothbrush. I check the dates. The recording is a record of plateaus that drop further into the abyss every three or four months till the tsunami of forgetfulness leaves her nowhere to drop. My darling father responds to the repetitive minutiae as if he has heard them afresh. Lost to herself, he allows her to remind herself of who she was. My father the furniture restorer was a haven and refuge for fragments, restoring wholeness, radiance and beauty to the damaged and the broken. A man whose grace and goodness under fire my mother never took for dullness. A man who took responsibility for his own life and the decisions he made – unlike his father, a feckless charmer whose throw of the dice dispensed a wife and discarded a son.

I skip to the two recordings near the end – the thief of who, what and where has come bringing silent stillness.

"Aren't you playing today, Una, darling?"

"Do I do that?"

"Yes, you do." Silence … "Here. I'll put your fingers where you need to start."

Suddenly, instead of fingers stroking keys, I hear a sound as unexpected as tropical rain that pelts against windowpanes and demands to break and enter. But this, this is the sound of my mother's hands hitting her head and bare skin in a terrifying clapping tempo that increases in ferocity. "No! … No! … *Stop.*" It is my father as I've never heard him before: an imperious voice full of angst. His voice morphs into soothing slowness, "You'll hurt yourself. I'm going to hold onto you very gently. That's right. You just rest your head on my shoulder. I'll stroke your hair. You like that." They are united in the ocean of their salted misery: his of loss and longing and hers of forgetfulness. Then he begins to sing softly to her, 'That's Amoré', but I sense his deep sorrow mired within its swaying rhythm. *Enough!* Without memory, there is no music. *That's enough for me today.* I am beginning to fill in the gaps in my mother's deterioration since I left three years ago. Tomorrow I will skip to the last few recordings.

Despite a nine-hour sleep, I greet the new day exhausted. Another day to face, when all I want is yesterdays long gone. I don't know if I can listen to much more of a past life and the small deaths within her, but I steel myself and switch the recording unit on. Classical FM plays in the background and above it is the slow, intermittent scrape of a spoon on the edge of a bowl. "Just another mouthful of porridge. You look like an adorable baby bird stretching its neck out waiting eagerly for the next mouthful. You must be starving." Fifteen minutes later, "Well done, my darling. All gone."

"Who am I?"

"You're my wife."

"*No, I'm not.* I'm your sister. You're Roland. On my seventh birthday you gave me a ballerina music box. It played 'Für Elise' ... You said its tempo suited me. Remember?"

With its simple harmonies and a light-hearted melody it became the first piece of music my mother learnt to play on the piano.

My father knows the story well, and he slips readily into his role in her reality. "Yes, I remember, Una. I said it was graceful and gliding like you, but I also said, 'Una, can't you learn to play something else other than that baguette by Earwig?' You were indignant. You reminded me it was a bagatelle and that it was disrespectful of me to call a genius like Ludwig van Beethoven, Earwig."

"Beethoven was almost deaf when he wrote 'Für Elise'. You forgot that, Roland." My mother starts to sob. Has she suddenly remembered that Roland, seven years older than her, died in a motorcycle accident when she was eleven? An unspoken-about tragedy in her family – the loss of what had been and what would never be. It had broken her parents' marriage; her father guilty in his grief for he had loaned Roland the money for the bike, and her mother unforgiving in her pain because he had done so despite her misgivings. My mother? Never one to flee from life, she chose to embrace its beauty alongside the terrifying and the unknowable.

She always played 'Für Elise' to commemorate Roland's birthday, each yearly rendition imbued with the intellectual challenge and improvisational flair of a new arrangement, so she wouldn't vex him in his afterlife as she had sometimes done in this. But there was, in all the pieces my mother liked to play, a melancholy, a longing that existed alongside the brightness-of-being within her.

In all of ten seconds her mind switches to birthdays, the fragment of connection to Roland gone. "Do you think my husband will be coming soon … it's my birthday, and I want to dance?" I hear her laugh and imagine her hands flowing in beautiful shapes as they always did when she was excited.

"He will. We better get you ready."

"Am I a nuisance?"

"No, *never*. You're a sweetheart. Let's find you a pretty dress, do your hair and make-up, and you'll be like Cinderella at the ball."

"*No* … go away! *I'm not Cinderella.* I want to stay at home. *Leave me alone!*"

How my father stays so calm. "I'm sorry I upset you, Una. I was trying to help."

He must carry such a heavy burden inside. When he used to speak to me on the phone, he always seemed oblivious to the magnitude of his ability to care.

"No one's going to take you away. Here will always be your home. Close your eyes, Una, and listen. What do you hear inside the room?"

"The grandfather clock."

"Yes. It's tick-tock and chimes will always remind you of where you are … at home. For everything else, I will always be there to remember for you."

"You are a good man. You're just like my husband."

"I am your husband, Una."

"Yes, you are, and you love me."

"We love one another very much."

I press the stop button on the recorder and put it down. Where did he learn his techniques to meet my mother's physical and emotional needs? Simple. He was a deeply loving man. That's all he needed to be able to validate, acknowledge and empathise. I'm face to face with the fact that there's a hardness in me that was neither in my mother nor is in my father. Is it a lack of patience or a throwback to a paternal family flaw?

I go to the kitchen and pour a Merlot into a large, bulbous, long-stemmed glass. I need to think about what is recorded and what is not and the gap between the two. The velvet-red of the wine caresses my mouth and suffuses my body with the fullness of black cherry and plum and the smoothness of Lindt dark chocolate balls. My body and mind mellow and calm. Slowly it comes to me … to protect my mother my father entered her reality. He knew not to torture her with the impossible task of travelling into his world. To protect me he altered reality for the self-same reason. It seemed like control at the time, almost exclusion – my stuff getting in the way again. He ensured that the times I saw and spoke to my mother were those when she was having a clearer day. He'd wait till my mother was back from the wasteland to the land of her smiling. The Land of 'Yes' and 'No' and 'Hi, sweetie'.

As her Alzheimer's progressed, and I rang from my new overseas placement in London, my father would say, "I won't disturb her now, Kate. Listen, she's about to play Chopin's 'Prelude in E Minor'. I'll leave the phone off the hook so you can listen. Just hang up when she's finished."

Such a simple haunting piece of light and dark that I know so well. My mother's favourite.

I top up my wine and begin the recording from where it left off. It's as if the unit has channelled my thoughts – Chopin's 'Prelude in E'. The first *b* saddens the *c* that follows. Reflective and tragic, it is a piece that goes from a place far away, to home. I close my eyes and listen. I see her right-hand curve, slow and elegant as a swan's neck as it strokes the keys of the Steinway baby grand. Her left relaxed as it caresses three notes, to the right's one. Gifted, she held all the music in her head. I cry as the music reaches its powerful climax and then, like me, moves away as if exhausted by emotion.

I didn't know it at the time, but it's becoming clear my father would be strategic with the days he rang me.

"Hello, baby girl, thought I'd ring for a quick catch-up while your mother's having her breakfast. She's having her favourite smoothie: banana, kefir yoghurt, spinach, blueberries, freshly ground linseed and one of Henrietta's eggs. Say hello to Kate, darling." With this prompt and a newly acquired effusiveness, my mother always said, "Hi, sweetie." It covered all bases.

"Father?"

"Yes."

"You must be exhausted. I'm thinking of …"

"No need, Kate … *Really* … I'm coping fine."

The smoothie? Well, I realise now, she couldn't swallow well anymore. I'm sure she protested at the toddler sippy cup. I know my father – he blended enough for two.

The tacked-together fragments of the fabric of her memory, unravelling patchwork connections of decaying threads. My father shouldered all this in loving silence as his beloved, unfixable wife disappeared before his eyes, and he before hers, with appalling irreversibility.

Why did my father not submit this tape in his defence? Atonement for his actions? Disdain for mercy-tempered justice? When he chose to end her suffering she was already too late for death with dignity, an easy death, a good death. Outsource, isolate, sedate? Abandon her to the anonymity and loneliness of a white cotton gown, a single room and a steel entry door that, as it secured, also imprisoned? He could not do it. She did not want it. She was sixty-one and, after eight years, he did not shirk what she had asked of him. He curtailed the vandal that pillaged and plundered from my mother the compass of place and time, autonomy of reasoning and judgment, the memory of loved ones and music itself. He did it in the time of the 'befores'.

Before she deteriorated into a vacated carapace. Unknowing. Unmoving. Unspeaking.

Before it strangled the automatic ease of breath itself.

Before complete invisibility.

My father released her knowing that Death, with insidious ferocity, had already come for my mother five years ago. It had come in time-lapse, lingered and placed her in a holding bay.

The jury's verdict was unduly harsh – a testimony to assumption. Smothering registered, along with my father's waxwork figure, shadowed eyes and hidden fault lines of grief, as too callous, too brutal. The last part of the tape tells it was not so. I hear 'Au Clair de la Lune' in the background.

"I cradle you dead. The colour of it is like your greying hair, the lack of animation, the cold …" He breaks down as fathomless, mournful sobs engulf him. In control of himself, he continues, "You opened your eyes for a flicker. I so needed to believe I saw a thank you in them. Your breath light, slow and sickly sweet. I held you in my arms, pressed against the pillow and my chest. The moonlight cradled us both. A light for lovers. A light for those who need to find their way in the dark. A light to follow into the river of illumination and warmth that is home. You will always be home to me, Una. Remember me to everyone, my darling."

I know what I must do.

When I visit my father in prison, it is one of those quiet days when the spring rain falls sweetly warm and the damp soil is redolent of new beginnings, of seeds stirring in the nourishing darkness pushing knowingly upward into the air and light. I am shocked when I see him. He is stooped and the timbre of his voice hoarse. I try to keep my thoughts from showing on my face. He keeps his hands beyond my sight, but when I hand him the Intention to Appeal I see the tremor in his left hand like an indecisive dragonfly. "With the evidence of the recordings, there are compelling grounds for an appeal to challenge the conviction. You just need to sign this." I see the look on his face. "Don't worry. It'll be a private affair. The Court of Criminal Appeal is a closed court; only three judges form the panel, and the majority view prevails. I've hired one of Australia's leading silks, Terry Winston, from Sir Owen Dixon Chambers. He's confident the conviction will be squashed, and you'll be acquitted on the spot. No need for a retrial."

"How confident, Kate?"

"I'd be betting my redundancy money on it, and that's a six-figure sum. In Terry's words, 'They'll decide it's not in the public interest when you were motivated wholly by love and compassion and your wife's wishes.' Basically, the original conviction will be considered unduly severe and oppressive in light of the new evidence."

He's hesitating. He diverts. "Redundant?"

"Yes, voluntary redundancy. Time to be there for you as you were for Mother. You have a shed full of furniture that needs restoring. I have a soft, enticing sales pitch and killer business acumen. Sign on the dotted line. What do you say?"

"You're sure about this, Kate?"

"Do I have a Montblanc pen, or what?"

He takes it and signs. *Yes!*

I hug him and say, "Father, I need you. I love you. I'm so sorry for what I didn't do."

As I embrace him, I can feel he has nothing more to give – I am hugging a husk. Now, it is time for me to banish the shadow of my paternal grandfather that follows me. My penance will be the soft voice, the steady hands and the heart that serves. For that, I am grateful.

ordered smoked salmon as a side when it needed bacon. My hunger and the explorer in me satisfied, I leave knowing I will never return.

After my appointment I go for an ocean swim on the incoming tide where the creek opens its mouth to the sea. Tucked around the corner from the main beach is a beach fit for three. It's a weekday and I have it all to myself. I stretch out on my towel and close my eyes. My sun-glowed skin's a recharging battery as gentle bejewelled glints flicker through the weave of my straw sunhat onto closed eyelids. My thoughts drift to a true story, long unrecalled but worth remembering. It carries me with it like the returning tide. It is the story of Little Buddha and Schmetterling.

Forty years ago (the eighties), my life and their story coincided over two elemental forces of nature – ice and lava. One, a spherical shrine of hollowed ice sheltering marinated shrimp with sea urchin and caviar, on a bed of sea lettuce. The other, a dessert with floating islands of fluffy hazelnut meringue lapped by pools of vanilla praline cream and marbled (when spoon breached meringue) by languid lava rivulets of raspberry and dark chocolate coulis.

Tekeshi and Theo. Their births separated by fifteen years and an ocean, their childhoods conjoined by isolation. Adulthoods guided by the call for fusion of culture, community and cuisine.

The Pacific Ocean calls, familiar and unfamiliar. Dunes and turtles fringe the coastal city where Tekeshi lives. Hamamatsu. A city charmed with a sixteenth-century castle, four hundred cherry trees and a cocktail-layered vista of white, blue and green. The mammoth Mount Fuji (four thousand metres tall, elegant and snow-capped) embraces what lies below like a friendly uncle. The area is culture and nature-rich – shrines, waterfalls, volcanic foothills and a linear landscape of rowed green plantations of green tea. In Utogi, wasabi grows in the sacred meltwaters from Mount Fuji that produce the clear streams of the Fuji, Oi and Abe Rivers. In Suruga Bay the rare, delicately sweet sakura shrimp float and scatter.

Tekeshi's family are rural people, and his favourite dish is gyoza: unassuming, yielding dumpling pockets whose feminine softness and warmth allow the attention of taste buds to the flavour and texture inside. Always, for Tekeshi, the soy to add tang and depth and local freshly-shaved wasabi which, to the unseasoned, naïve eater, sears the nostrils and make the eyes water. Who could not help but smile after a comforting belly full of gyoza? The known means little to Tekeshi. What tugs at him, like a child wanting attention, is the call of the *unknown* – a desire to experience a foreign fusion of bush and city. His parents with their *umeboshi* (sour plum) faces and toil-hardened, veined hands cannot understand this desire in their only child and, because they do not understand, he is not close to them. Their outlook on life is like the dumpling without the filling. No tang of soy sauce. No heat of the wasabi. Not wanting an answer, they ask him in Japanese, "Why do you go?"

The sharp slap of silence.

"You stop your studies, and you will be alone with no money and no job."

Their words will change nothing.

Tekeshi, in between his business management studies, works early mornings and late nights as a kitchen porter in a hotel. He saves enough to qualify for a twelve-month Working Holiday Visa in Australia. He is twenty.

It is five-thirty p.m. in Sydney, the time when daylight skulks slowly away under the slate-grey of early evening. It's the hiatus between the day's mix of the ordinary and the evening's diverse incomings of the bright and the tarnished; the slick and the refined; the feather-bowered and the sequined; the addled, addicted and androgynous; the bisexuals, metrosexuals and transsexuals; the bohemians, cross-dressers, models, socialites and paper bag metholholics. This nocturnal family of the fun-hungry (apart from the methoheads) will queue in long snaking lines to enter the burnt orange, sage green and cream Art Deco building that stands majestically on the corner of the nightclub precinct. All of them drawn, in order of importance, by sex, theatre, food, art and politics.

On the opposite corner is the real estate office of Ari Finkler. Theo Nilsson has popped in for a hi-and-bye catch-up.

"Mazel tov on your latest venture, Theo. Restaurant, nightclub, cabaret theatre, bar, brasserie. You heff no fear. You open more restaurants than most people heff sex."

"I think you need to speak to your wife about that one, Ari. The average is once a week. I know you're a true gentleman, but it would help if you told her to *shtup* regularly." It's an in-joke. Theo was highly amused the day he discovered something that sounded like *shut up* meant *to have sex* in Yiddish.

"Better now I tell you a joke, Theo. Heff I told you de one about Simon?"

"You probably have, Ari, but they're always worth a third hearing, old chap."

"It's Simon's ninetieth birthday. Miriam stands at de bedroom door in a new negligee. She dims the light, and says, 'Heff I got sumtink for you, Simon – Super Sex.' He replies, 'Vunderful. Denk you, darlink. I'll heff de soup.' You shake your head, Theo. Tomorrow I have new joke for you."

Theo worries about Ari's repetitive repertoire of jokes always full of hyperbole and nuanced complaint. Ari worries about Theo's *big plans*. Plans with the grand vision, impulsivity and foolhardiness of an alcoholic. For all his brilliance as a chef, Theo is a *lechen kopt* – a noodlehead – when it comes to business. Still, his evangelical zeal, passion, kindness and warm-hearted chutzpah make strangers feel like family and rarely fail to draw sponsors and business partners. Ari knows. He is one of them. He has a half-share in the corner building across the road. Poor Theo, thinks Ari. Sometimes wrong place, wrong time. The man has as much introspection as a Jack Russell.

Tekeshi arrives at Sydney airport. Booking an airport shuttle is still too demanding for his low-level English. He sticks with the simplicity of what he knows – trains. He has no plan where to alight. He's already run into trouble asking a person who has an inner seat next to them, "Prease, may I shit?" Ignored, he wonders if this culture knows little about politeness.

St James station. The train empties. Tekeshi takes this as his cue; besides, it's the third stop and three is his lucky number. Once in daylight, he's at the place where concrete paths act as compass points as they corral one of the oldest parks in Australia. He marvels at the wide-open space, the lush grass surrounded by buildings and busy roads with relays of buses. He sits on a bench and contentedly soaks up the last of the late afternoon sun's rays then, as the sun sinks, wanders towards a large and impressive fountain. He wonders if it has carp. No carp.

Instead, a six metre, pedestalled, bronze statue of a lean, muscular youth whose right arm extends protectively and in his left a stringed musical instrument. Beneath the figure, water falls from the nostrils of horse heads into tri-levelled granite basins and from there into a pool of stone dolphins and tortoises who expel jets of water. A god. A goat. A goddess and her stag. A drawn sword and a horned beast.

Tekeshi waits till the light fades and the magic of floodlights illuminate. He marvels at the detail and the scale of the fountain but prefers the works of Akio Makigawa whose contemporary sculptures capture the elemental forces of nature with tranquil stillness and dynamism. Sculptures not to subdue or impress but to invite connection and contemplation.

He wanders through the park and takes the path that leads him to an easterly road. It seems the one most likely to lead him away from the hubbub and expensive hotels.

Theo gone, Ari Finkler is about to close shop and set the alarms. Already the chill of the night air insinuates, biting into the lingering warmth left by the air-con. He's about to switch the lights off when he sees, in the transparent space between the ads, the smooth, round-as-a-ball face of a man with small set eyes with single-edged eyelids – another Japanese tourist lost without translation. Ari watches with amusement as the eyes scour, first the 'For Sale' and then 'To Let'. The man looks placidly puzzled as he draws up the zippered collar of his black anorak. Ari waits for the zeros to drop.

A mild panic rises in Tekeshi's chest. He realises everything in the window has too many zeros for his wallet. *Where is he going to stay tonight?*

Ari taps on the window and beckons him in. "Hello, I'm Ari Finkler."

"Herro, my name Tekeshi Tanaka."

"You look like you need help."

"Justa momentu prease …" He tries to repeat Ari's words. "Ooh rooko rike–"

"Vait. Vait," Ari interrupts in staccato. Ari draws a giant question mark in the air with his index finger, shrugs his shoulders and places both palms upwards from bent arms, his eyes wide and his brow furrowed. Tekeshi yawns, tilts his head to the right and places his hands in prayer position against his right cheek. Then, he does the most unexpected and outrageous thing of all. He closes his eyes as a series of snores rattle from his nose and throat in a sleep apnea duet. *Somewhere to sleep.* Ari, caught between comprehension and astonishment, bellows with laughter and immediately knows he likes this man and his innocent, happy energy. Tekeshi slowly opens one eye and smiles a smile of the understood. Ari's already thought of a nickname for him: Little Buddha.

"You tourist?"

"One more."

"Holiday? Verk Visa?

"Yesu … horidy walk bisa. Back Tokyo, walk hoteru."

Ari knows where he is going to take him. To someone whose familial, supportive, embracing mentorship needs a kitchen porter, "You vill please come mit me."

Ari and Little Buddha cross the road with the same technique: find a gap in the two-way lanes, walk in a brisk straight line, look straight ahead. Those who waiver end up humiliated, maimed or dead. Cornered by the constant honk and hum of two roads, and abutted by buildings either side, is a two-storey Art Deco building with two façades, one facing south, the other east. Tekeshi and Ari appraise the building very differently.

Ari knows it well. On his books for an eight-figure sum eighteen months before, he and Theo own a fifty-per cent share each. In its heyday it would have listed as POA – Price On Application. Apart from the incredible twelve-foot-high ceilings and an impressive central foyer that rises two storeys, he dislikes the building: it is an ill-matched mishmash of styles. Due to a lack of maintenance, unsympathetic aluminium re-placements embarrass the original 1930s arched, double-hung windows with timber sashes. Blocked-in second floor windows shame the decorative mouldings from the 1950s. The latest addition to the first floor, a cantilevered balcony with a timber deck and toughened clear glass, is the final act of vandalism.

Ari thinks, *Oy vey! Oy vey!* But he says, "You like? Beautiful?"
Tekeshi nods politely, "Byuutifuru."

What Tekeshi sees is quite different. He sees beyond the
building to the flow of energy around it. He sees it as an island
and the roads as rivers whose speed has cutting energy, a place
of business bound by the power of two roadways forming
an L-shape that attracts a steady stream of people, but all of
them burdened by petty troubles. The southern second-storey
windows have their eyes blinded, board replaces glass. No
looking outside. No looking within.

The building's entrance faces east and above the doorway
on the stucco is a sign in substantial neon letters – ABELLAS.
A broad, hedged pedestrian walkway that hides the road from
sight, but not sound, is a functional solution lacking in elegance. Overall, Tekeshi knows Abellas will be a place where
the money is tidal – difficulties and struggles in forming a
solid business footing. Easy beginnings. Difficult continuings.
The building's street number contains two threes and an eight.
$3 + 3 + 8 = 14$ and $1 + 4 = 5$. Five means prosperity will flow
but also agitation and bad luck. The man who owns this has
come for growth and validation but also to find inner peace
and balance. An old Japanese proverb pops into Tekeshi's
head. He who runs after two hares will catch neither.

As Ari and Tekeshi enter the foyer, each feels the dramatic
impact of space and largess. Wide fluted cornices border the
twelve-foot ornate geometric ceiling. A leadlight Art Deco
sun rises two-storeys through the centre of the foyer and is
flanked, on the wall either side, by a seven-foot Artes-style

bronze sculpture of a dancer and an outrageously large colourful advert for the 1985 Sydney Gay Mardi Gras.

"It's wow. Yes?"

"Wao," repeats Tekeshi, but the bold, geometric diamonds, the triangles and the angular lines unsettle him. They look like shards and spear-tips meant to cut and slice.

The foyer's amber-glass doors lead to a lift that they take to the first floor. As they alight a door faces them. It belongs to a small two-bedroom flat, a modification to allow the head-chef to sleep over on the busiest nights that finish for patrons at one-thirty in the morning and for him with sunrise, the last of the previous night's wine and then, bed. The door is slightly ajar, and Ari calls out, "Schmetterling, come and meet Little Buddha."

Theo and an oversize glass of a 1978 Chateau Latour come to the door. He is still in his head chef's white and black. "Ari, old chap, will you stop calling me that. The word sounds like something that could do serious damage."

Theo is wary of any of Ari's *schm* words as, apart from *schmetterling,* they are all pejoratives: *schmutzig* (dirty), *schmuck* (self-made fool, aka dick), *schmoe* (a stupid person), *schmoppet* (a charming puppet with a limited vocabulary).

"Vell, my old friend, I promise dat ven you stop acting like a butterfly." The reference is to Theo's signature yellow bow tie, alongside his compulsive flits from one new restaurant venture to another seeking the nectar of success.

"His real name, Ari?"

"Tekeshi."

Theo turns to Tekeshi and bows slightly. He knows Ari's brought him another kitchen hero. The man deserves a finder's fee. "Hello, I'm Theo. Nice to meet you."

"Me too."

It's an exchange between two faces whose default position is generosity and warmth.

"Why don't you work for me?"

"One more prease."

Theo realises it's the 'don't' that has confused him. He points, "*You*. Work for *me*."

"Ah, yesu! I walk you."

Theo waves them both inside. "Here's a red for you Ari. Tekeshi?

"No, prease."

Ari swirls and sniffs the red as he holds the large, rounded bowl by the stem, but he's not concentrating on the scent or the closing note of the wine's aroma. He takes a small sip and allows it to roll around on his tongue for a moment. "I em vundering–"

"Wondering if it's okay if he could stay here in the second bedroom till he's on his feet," Theo adds before Ari can finish.

"You know me too vell, my friend."

"Look, Ari, old chap, you've always been a person of small kindnesses. Without you at boarding school, at the age of six, I'd have been lobster mousse within a day."

Ari raises his glass, "L'chayim, chaver. To life, my friend."

"To life and friendship, Ari. To you too, Tekeshi."

Within two weeks Tekeshi has mastered the rhythm of a professional kitchen. He's preemptive, strategic, quick on his feet, spatially aware and energetic. He's cool around heated chefs and cookpots and on top of everything: speed of cleaning pots, pans and tools and homing them in the right place so they're ready to go. The floor is spotless. Food is peeled and chopped with lightning precision and the needs of the various chefs preempted. Theo and the kitchen staff have created a nickname for him. Ninja Octopus.

Teasing Tekeshi eases the pressure in the kitchen. He gives as good as he gets.

"Where is the butter, Tek?"

"Re/frig/er/a/tor."

"What do you need to do with the cake?"

"Dekorehshan keki."

Then, there's his pronunciation of McDonalds (Ma/kudo/na/ru/do), and the light banter finds the larrikin in him, and he shouts out alongside the kitchen staff and chefs, "Oi. Oi. Oi." It's a refrain that crosses seamlessly between national borders. Seemingly unpronounceable Japanese words to the Western eye and tongue – *tsutaerarenakatta* (couldn't tell), *occhokochoi* (clumsy) and *atatakakunaketta* (wasn't warm) – redress the balance of vocal incompetencies.

Curious and watchful as well as playful, Tekeshi pinpoints Theo's style: respectful to the rhythm of the seasons; pure, clean flavours; bold and exotic combinations and brilliantly aesthetic platings. All the dishes have a casually absolute elegance and joy. Theo is equally watchful. Within six months he asks Tekeshi, "I want to introduce a new selection to the pre-theatre degustation menu. Sushi. Are you okay to do that, Tekeshi? Samples by the end of the month."

"Mmm. No problem,"Tekeshi says with calm assuredness, as the first step in his plan does not include washing dishes forever, but he's thinking, *why people berieve if you Japanese, you eat sushi, you make it?* He has done neither. His calm exterior betrays none of the flutters he feels in his chest. Flutters like a small bird trapped in a bamboo cage.

It's fifteen months since Theo opened Abellas as head chef and part-owner. He is peeling under the pressure of the physical challenge of a 19/6 week that feels like 24/7, the rigid schedules, the responsibility, the unknown, the financial risk. He feels trapped. The puritan in him reaches for the hedonist to relieve the drive for perfection, to drown the fear of not being good enough, of tumbling from the firmament of his restaurant's coveted three hats and of being voted Restaurant of the Year but with only one of the three possible hats.

First comes the Grand Marnier – the remnants left in a bottle after the night's souffles. When there is not enough in the bottle, another is opened. Unlike red wine, Theo is not improving with time. His structural faults are maintained and accentuated. His favourites increase from Bollingers at two hundred dollars a bottle to Jean-Louis Chave Hermitages at five hundred. Until the night he opens his cellar's most expensive bottle, a Gros Père et Fils, Grand Cru Richebourg. Seven thousand dollars. He begins to argue with himself.

Sober: *Oh no, Theo.* You'll go broke.

Sloshed: *So what?* Highs and lows. Penury's never permanent.

Sober: *You're an alcoholic!* Admit it, old chap, you need help.

Sloshed: *Bugger off!* I'm a dignified, disinclined to violence, drunk.

Sober: *How the hell would you know?* You can't remember what you did last night.

Drinking buddies: "It'll be OK, mate. Have a drink."

Theo's committed to three packets of unfiltered Camels a day, each cigarette fourteen milligrams of tar and one milligram of nicotine. His day begins with three cigarettes when he's half-asleep and still in bed as he thinks about the day ahead. Another cigarette when he goes to the loo and then, one after showering.

Tekeshi no longer lives in the flat, so he's not witness to the squatters scattered like knocked-over skittles: bottles of wine partially and fully emptied. Spills next to the bed and on the coffee table, and an overflow of empties in sink and bin, further betray Theo. As alcohol is nothing without food, and food nothing without alcohol, the debris from slices of truffle on croutons and artisanal blue cheeses on fig and olive specialty crackers means Theo's a pre-poster boy for AA and Weight Watchers.

What Tekeshi does notice when they are together in the restaurant kitchen is Theo's aftershave: a pungent mix of kitchen, alcohol and tobacco. Theo's, "Fix it", reprimands to the other chefs when platings are not up to standard are frayed and inconsistent. His bow tie is having a nervous breakdown. It no longer sits flat and central. It's skewered and its left-top corner buckles under a wayward collar. On the worst of days, it's a crumpled origami butterfly salvaged from a wastepaper bin. Theo's hair, already delicate, is thinning on top like wisps of wind-blown candyfloss. That his socks don't match is not a fashion statement. Overall, he has the wayward look of an absent-minded professor.

Tekeshi has the deep calm of a fisherman, but he is unable to lead Theo by example: tai chi, relaxing breathing techniques, meditation and fishing. Theo is too driven – all movement, and no space. Worried for Theo, Tekeshi, at the end of one of his shifts, pops across the road to see Ari. He takes with him a few samplers he's been experimenting with on his days off. A miniature tuna tart with mustardy wasabi and ginger and carpaccio of scallop on top of foie gras, with citrus dressing.

"Thenk you. Tek a seat. Always gutt to see you, Little Buddha, food or no food."

"I hope you like. Prease, I ask you something?"

"Sure. Vat is it?"

"Ari, I worry about Theo. He is Shinkansen – bullet train." He tells Ari about the tell-tale bow tie.

"My father hed daily ritual. He began de day by making his bed perfectly. He never missed a morning. I dink he vas honouring his day – *If my bed is neat, my day vill be calm and ordered.* Even ven very sick he still made it, but it was never as neat. One day, I am looking into his room, and de bed is not made. Dat day I grieve de most."

Tekeshi honours the silence that follows. He gives Ari time to bring himself into the present.

"Little Buddha, neither of us can put de kibosh on it. He is Mister Perpetual Motion."

"What makes him this?"

"Can't help it. To stop is pain. De pain of regret, guilt and fear for past failures and those he feels he has let down. Mebbe he needs a therapist. He's alvays been ahead of his time, more artist and innovator than businessman. Dat's vhy he admires and respects you, Tekeshi. You heff all three."

The day after the sushi directive, Tekeshi wakes with a plan. Over the ensuing weeks he samples fifty dishes at the top ten sushi trains: Double Bay, Five Dock, Coogee, Randwick, Chatswood. He watches the chefs slice, dice, roll, cook and sculpt. Within the month, he presents Theo with a seven-dish degustation menu with a suggested set-price of one hundred and twenty-five dollars. He's also been working on two spectacular dishes at home. One *umami* (savoury), one *amai* (sweet). Both are innovative and elegantly spectacular – *ice and lava*. Tekeshi spends weeks perfecting each delicate, gentle freezing and each chocolate and raspberry rivulet. The two surprise dishes are to match the theme of an upcoming theatre booking: the show, *Elemental*. Theo has entertainment nightly in the restaurant, brasserie and cocktail bar. Tekeshi marvels at his generosity. He's given the theatre booking to a local dance company for a couple of months to help with their cash flow, to rescue them from liquidation.

At midnight, at the end of the first trial evening of the sushi-inspired degustation menu, Theo calls Tekeshi into the restaurant to a round of applause. "To Tekeshi, the master of small things."

At that moment, Tekeshi knows he has found his *ikigai* – his purpose in life.

Theo continues, "No more sink for you, Ninja Octopus. You are now Chef de Partie. Many chefs start in the kitchen. I did myself. In another six months when you finish here, I want you to work for GC's restaurant, Amicus. He's the one that's put Hobart on the gastronomic map. You'll love it. You'll love Tasmania. Pristine waters, fertile soil and an untouched landscape. It's a place above and beyond organic."

Six years and over one thousand kilometres and the Tasman Sea have separated Tekeshi and Theo, but it does not diminish their deep friendship. Tekeshi is now head chef of his own restaurant – Buddha's Butterfly.

Built into the rock face, the architecture and the landscape meld as one. In a riverside setting on the bend of a deep estuary, the building is invisible from a distance. As patrons arrive by a small wooden private ferry they see Buddha's Butterfly appears like a mirage. The approach clears the mind. It whispers with the balm of a soft breeze, "Leave the chaos and pressure of the outside world behind."

Inside, there are no white box interiors. Sculptures by Makigawa intersperse the raw natural space. The chopsticks are freshly cut bamboo and are cool in the hands, the lacquerware is warm and the hand-thrown rice bowls feather-light. Day or night, the restaurant holds a subtle, elegant Zen ambience. The restaurant's floor-to-ceiling window embraces the full magnificence of a Japanese garden designed to be viewed on the diagonal and seen optimally from a seated position. Space and scale are transformed, from the hundred-metre mark beyond the garden, by borrowed landscape from a dense and rugged white-trunked bushland tangle of eucalypts.

It is the time of year when day and night are in equal measure. Autumn. Shadow and light, picture and poem, the outside is living art: the glowing golds, rusty reds and ochre orange of autumnal maples; the yellow, copper, bronze and red of Japanese elms; tresses of languorous willows; slender and smooth feathery bamboo; untormented pines and the dark limbs of plum trees. Moss blankets the earth instead of grass, and lichen mottles the large, grey stone boulders planted with pleasing random asymmetrical precision. The air is so pure, it is scentless. Its chill forewarns that winter is fast approaching. Yellow, orange, white and red brocaded koi glide and gleam in the pure spring-fed stream that flows westward. A waterfall and a cascade, half-hidden in the shade, flow with a hypnotic rhythm of murmurs and whispers. At night the water catches the magic of the moon's reflection to an audience of hushed voices and muted background music.

Tonight, the clouds blanket the refrigerated air. The nature of change means nothing lasts forever. Winter will soon strip bare, and the lilting mournful trill of the cuckoo will die till its summer return. Tekeshi waits. Waits for the call he knows will come. He waits as a silvery, silent mist settles, turning the visible, invisible. It is not a call that arrives but a telegram. A telegram from Ari – *Theo's weak. Come see him*

ASAP. Tekeshi takes the first flight. Within three hours he is at Theo's bedside.

Theo opens his eyes for a moment and looks at Tekeshi. Tekeshi takes his hand, and in a gentle voice he says, "You are, and will always be, in every dish I make." They look at each other. Tekeshi smiles but only Theo's eyes speak a smile because his mouth cannot. Death clouds his eyes. Tekeshi will remember Theo's death as *karoshi*, death by a dark word. Overwork. Theo is forty-five.

Sun-dried and sandy I trace my path back to my car on the headland. The waves frill and curl gently to the beach and glide bubble-edged across the moist glazed sand where earth meets water and water meets the azure of the endless sky. I ask myself, why now? Why now, did this story whisper to be told? It called to remind me of what I am not. I am not: the no song of a bird that will not return; the no of the tea that disappointed; the no of the salmon instead of the bacon or the no of unartful plating. It called to remind me of what I am. I am the yes of the vital missing ingredient, a friend to share a spontaneous moment in connection, laughter and banter. That, yes that, would have made all the difference to the start of my day.

Searching for North

A NOVELLA

Polar north can't get away from a magnet; the magnet finds it, no
matter what.

Handle with Care
Jodi Picoult

Lying in the gutter
I cut the cord from my mother.
So, pat me on the head and say
Go to sea boy, get to sea man.
'Gutter Black'

Hello Sailor

Searching for North

"Well, I've got an idea," said Rabbit, "and here it is. We take Tigger for a long explore, somewhere where he's never been, and we lose him there, and next morning we find him again, and – mark my words – he'll be a different Tigger altogether."

"Why?" said Pooh.

"Because he'll be a Humble-Tigger ... a sad Tigger, a Melancholy Tigger, and Oh, Rabbit I-am-glad-to-see-you Tigger. That's why."

"I should hate him to go on being Sad," said Piglet. Doubtfully.

"Tiggers never go on being Sad," explained Rabbit.

The House at Pooh Corner
A. A. Milne

ZERO

Once upon a Tuesday at four-forty in the morning, close to the winter solstice, the boy is born.

It is the month when the whales – the male and female humpbacks to breed and female southern rights to birth – leave the chilly Antarctic waters to travel north with the eastern current of the Great Southern Land, to the calm, tropical shallows of the Pacific. The polished ultramarine sky, the twenty-degree ocean waters and the binoculared visitors on the easterly projecting clifftop wait. Those on the clifftop wait, with patient hope, for glimpses of the unseen tonnage that glides below the deep waters of the wintery sea. They wait for the acrobatics of tail flukes, the three-metre blows and the majestic breeches, which rise like seedlings out of the water, then slap down with the power of felled cedar.

Secluded, quiet and commanding, a hospital sits on the clifftop. Its name, Mona, is Celtic for 'high born'. Northerly, and to the east, high rugged rocky ridges jut out in the sea as a lengthy line of sandhills cower, and the beach ends abruptly. Turbulent waters curl, dash, moan and roar. The breeze from the ocean is fierce and sharp.

In the delivery room of the maternity wing of the hospital, a woman applies a repertoire of birthing strategies. First, control of breath as a steady three-in, three-out. Then the cervix visualised as a pond into which a pebble creates ever-widening circles as she squats, back to the wall, pummelling her thighs to divert her brain from the torment of contractions. Finally, on the delivery table, she bears down on her hands and knees to widen her pelvic outlet. Still he does not come.

Despite the cramped confines, the baby prefers the comfort of the known to the unknown: the reassuring stability of amniotic fluid at body temperature; the ease of breath and nutrients without effort; the hypnotic regularity of his mother's heartbeat alongside digestion's rumblings and blood flow's gurgles and, beyond the fleshy walls, the gentle hum of the outside world.

Forbidden to push further, the woman rests momentarily. The obstetrician won't allow her to continue bearing down. "You're fully dilated, but his head is large. You've done your best – an eight-hour labour is a good day's work." Gas and forceps and the baby is out.

The discharge papers state, 'Wrigley lift out'. The mother takes this to mean one of three things: the baby, worm-like, protested; it is the gynecological equivalent of a Heimlich manoeuvre or, least likely, chewing gum was involved.

A photo of the baby at four days shows him still in denial of the cold chaos and bright lights: elbows bent; hands, curled fists; eyes closed tight.

His parents already know what they will name him. Alexander. A perfect name for the single-syllable surname, Hedd. Perfect for two other reasons. One, it holds no ammunition for bullies in its shortening as Richard would. No … no one would knowingly place that life burden on a child. Two, it means defender and helper of humanity. His mother hopes he will become a capable compassionate man of character. She does not wish greatness upon him. Alexander the Great? *No.* She does not want him to bear the burden of half the known world and dead by thirty-two. She sandwiches Leon, her father's name, between Alex and Hedd. Her brother and sister have no children. The boy will be her father's only grandson.

THREE

I'm three. I know 'bout mirrors. Ben doesn't. He thinks there are two of him. He kisses the mirror.

"No," says Ma, "he thinks it's another budgie. He's pecking it because he wants to be the only one."

I'm not the only one. There's someone *exactedly* like me.

"Glad to meet ya! Name's Tigger. T-l-double guh-er! That spells Tigger!"

He's a bouncer like me. I bounced before I walked. Ma showed me a photo. I am in a Jolly Jumper. Ma should bounce. Her tummy is a balloon. Ma says bouncing isn't good for babies. Soon I will have a Baby Roo like Tigger. I will say to Mum, "Buy malt." Babies like malt.

Tigger climbs trees. He is fun, fun, fun. He is more than me. Five – like my best friend B. Ma says Tigger is just like me. "Why is he?"

Ma holds up her fingers. "One – he has no fear. Two – he never gives up. Three – he is always cheerful. Four – he wants to be helpful. Five – he is sure he can do *anything*." Then she laughs and says, "You're both a handful but so lovable." She kisses me two times. I hug her leg.

Tigger and me are Masked Avengers. Protectors of the Forest. Champion of the Underdog. I ask Ma what is under a dog that needs help. I know they like tummy rubs.

"Alex, an underdog is anyone who needs help because they never win races or the prize in pass the parcel."

I watch Tigger on TV. I have a cape and a big sunhat with a feather. Ta-dah, I am Tigger. Then I wait for Da. I look at the clock. At the five Da is home. Me, Ma and Da go to the living room. Da swings me on a broom. I fly from sofa to sofa. I must save Croc, my soft toy, from falling.

Ma says, "Oh, help me, Mister Avenger." She's 'tending to be Croc.

Da says, "Have no fear, citizens. Masked Offender to the rescue."

Croc is safe now.

Ma says, "Thank you, Mister Avenger."

I say, "No need for thanks citizens. Masked Avenger away." That's eight words. Ma says I have a good brain. "Why do walnuts look like a brain?"

"They are good for the brain, Alex."

She says that to make me eat them. Yuck. The bestest nuts sound like a sneeze. Yum!

Tigger really, really likes malt. Ma says it is sweet, but we don't have any.

"We have the 'alt that begins with an 's'. Would you like a spoonful of that, Alex?"

I know that letter – S. S-alt. "Eugh!"

She laughs.

Tigger would like Ma. Ma doesn't like Rabbit and Eeyore. Just like me. Rabbit is mean. He wants to lose Tigger in the forest. I lost my fav'rite bear. He is still sad and lost. I miss him. Eeyore is no fun. He is always sad. "Ma, can Tigger sleepover?"

"The Hundred Acre Wood is a very long way from here. We will have to write to him."

I write on top of her letters. It is very col'ful. I drawed a picture of me in my Tigger pyjamas – black and orange. I stick the stamp on. Da shakes his head. He tells Ma it's a *ridikicerous* thing to do. It is a Tigger word – he sounds like

Rabbit. She says it would be *terribble* not to. That's a Tigger word too – Ma sounds like Pooh.

Da is nice *and* mean. At the park with B, Ma buys me and B the same ice-cream. Not Da. He gives B blue paper money. I get a big gold circle. It makes me sad *and mad*. I think Da likes B better. B is like Pooh.

I don't like Ma and Da mad. They are loud. I want to say, "Scuse me, p'ease shut up."

Da upsets Ma 'bout seatbelts and bike hats. Today Da says Alex is diff-i-cult and s'oilt. Ma says he is wrong. "Alex is s'irited. He's not a dog." Woof. Woof. I can be a dog. I wish I had a dog. And baby ducks. A farm came to preschool. I sat in a circle. All the baby ducks runned to me. One hid under my jacket. I am a magnet. Magnets are magic. I am magic with animals.

I can be loud. I yell and cry in the sup'market. I want a toy car. Ma always says, "No, Alex." I never give up … I am Tigger. At home, Da rolls me in the rug. At first I wobble like a worm. It's fun. I get out. I am still mad. Ma calls it *Da's Last Resort*. Once I taked a toy car. Ma said, "Sometimes kids do that, but it is wrong. We must take it back."

"Were you a Sometimes Kid?"

"I was, Alex. But my mum and dad taught me it was the wrong thing to do."

"What did you take?"

"A bar of chocolate from the sweet shop. Okay, Alex. Let's go."

"Will the lady yell?"

"No. Just say sorry and she will thank you for bringing it back. I have an idea–"

"A Tigger one?"

"No, a Pooh one. You must promise *never, ever* to do it again, *and I promise* to buy you a treat when the day's date has a one and a three in it. Okay?"

"Yes."

I can count to ten. Ma has four wooden blocks. Two have numbers on. She plays with them eberyday day. Today she's made Sat 23 May. I wish two was one. I look every day. One morning, it's Sun 31 May. I am happy like the sun.

I have a house on the sundeck. Ma made it from a big box. It has a table and two chairs. I have a little box that says M A I L. Every day I look in the box. Then, ta-dah, Tigger's letter. Ma sits on the floor in my house. She reads it to me.

Hello, buddy boy,

I love sleepovers – they're sleepericous. I babysit Roo because Kanga is busy. There are lots of villians in the Hundred Acre Wood doing suspicerous things. I am very sorry. I can't come. The Hundred Acre Wood is a very, very, very, very long way away.

Don't be sad. I have an idea to make you smile.

I will send you a card on your birthday and you can send me one on mine. My birthday is the same month as Christmas – so you won't forget.

Keep on doing what you do best.

Your bestest buddy,

Tigger.

PS. Just remember, Tigger and Alex don't stay sad for long. TTFN. Tigger Away!

"How will he know?"

"Your birthday?"

"Umm."

"Do not fear, citizen, Ma to the rescue. I will write a letter to him."

FOUR

I was three. I wake up. I am four – ta-dah.

"Happy Birthday, Mister Four," say Mum and Dad. They give me a high five.

"Fank you. Am I growed up now?"

"No," says Mum, "not till you need all your fingers *and toes* to count how old you are."

I look at my fingers and toes. "Will you be dead like Grandpa and Grandma?"

"Certainly not, but Dad and I will be a little bit wrinkly."

"Like an e'phant?"

Mum says, "No, not saggy and baggy like an elephant. Just a little wrinkly like the ends of your fingers when you stay in the bath too long."

Dad chases me round the TV room. His arm is like an e'phant trunk. He swings me up on his back and gives me a ride. It's fun. "More. Again. Again."

"Alex, I need a rest. You sit here, and I'll bring us a drink and a cookie."

I wait.

Oh, I forgetted. Mum had a baby on Fursday. Four sleeps before my birthday. She had her for breakfast, like me. Dad says no, *before* breakfast. A girl. She is zero. I call her Nattie. But it's really Nat-a-lie. I like it when her hands hold my finger. She is cute. Mum says I am a big brother now. I tell Mum I will show Nattie how to win races. If I win pass the parcel I will give her my prize. Mum says, "Nattie is lucky to have you for a brother."

I help Mum change the nappy sometimes. Wee'd nappies are very heavy. "Did Alex have bum bum nappies?"

"Yes, you did. I have a story about you and a nappy."

"Tell me. *Tell me!*" My mum likes stories. She tells me 'bout when I was little. I love stories 'bout me.

"Well, one Sunday when you were two we went to the beach with Dad. You would not take off your nappy. You went into the water with it. When you came out it was so full of water it was falling past your bottom. Still, you would *not* take it off. Then ta-dah! The next day, you decided never to wear a nappy ever again. And that's the story of *Alexander and the Very, Very Sandy, Soggy, No Good Nappy.*"

"I didn't do that."

"Oh yes, you did."

"Don't tell Vili that." I can say my V's now. I don't call Vili 'B' anymore. Vili is from Tonga. He has five sisters.

"I won't. Pinky promise."

Guess what? Babies don't do much. They are like *The Very Hungry Caterpillar,* 'cept stinky. I know a new word – cocoon.

It rhymes with balloon. Mum's tummy was a cocoon for me and Nattie.

I play with Nattie sometimes.

Peekaboo.

One potato, two potatoes, three …

Round and round the garden like a teddy bear …

Nattie likes peekaboo best. She is not bouncy like me and Tigger. She is bendy.

After my cookie and milk, Dad says, "Come on, Alex. Mum must make the things for your party. Let's go out with Nattie. Take your bike."

My bike is two years old. I ridded it everywhere. The back-pedal stops my bike. Dad says I am amazing. I can do skids, wheelies and sidekicks. Sidekicks are my favourite because the back-wheel slides out.

Bushy Place is near us. It looks like the Hundred Acre Wood but shrinked. It's a tangly place. The road is quiet and makes a U. I ride in front of Dad and Nattie. Faster and faster I go. The air wooshes on my face. I go so fast until I can't see them. Suddenly, I am Humpty Dumpty bumpety, bumpety never put back together again. On the way home, Da tells me not to tell Mum.

"Why?"

"Mum will be mad 'cos I took you riding without a helmet."

I don't tell Mum. I don't like fights.

At bedtime I ask Dad, "Tell me the story again, Dad. The Humpty Dumpty bumpety, bumpety story."

"Well, it is a dark and gloomy night–"

"*Dad*, not that story. Stop being silly."

"Well, it is a Sunday and we go for a birthday morning adventure with your sister. I take her in the stroller because she is too young to walk. The houses on the left are down a very, very steep slope and have no fences. The road has no kerb. There is no concrete path. Suddenly, you disappear. You and your bike have ridden off the road into the place where danger lurks. The bike is going faster and faster."

"Like in Pooh."

"You mean, 'Through the peaceful countryside raced the highness carriage. Faster and faster the coachman drove, for he knew out there was the most dreaded of them all' ... a plate glass window from the ground to roof."

"Yes, but not the end bit."

"You cannot not stop the bike because you are going too fast and your feet are bouncing off the pedals."

"Oh, I wish my feet were not so bouncy."

"No, Alex. It wasn't your feet that were bouncy, it was the bike. Anyway, there is a metal railing and a set of concrete steps. Don't look, I say to myself, don't look!"

"Why?"

"I am scared of what is about to happen."

"To my bike?"

"No, to *you*. I make myself look. Somehow you miss the railing. Your feet bounce off the pedals as you whizz down the steps. At the bottom of the steps, just ten metres away, a tall glass window. You are heading straight for it. You try to get your foot on the back-brake pedal. It bounces off. You try a second time. A third time. With each step, it bounces off. Faster and–"

"Faster than a speeding bullet?"

"Yes. I make myself look. You only have two seconds to do something. One … Two… *Thank the heavens!* Your feet find the pedal. You jam it hard, a sidekick into a sliding skid, lay the bike down and come to a halt. You pull it off just a metre from the glass."

"What did you say to me?"

"Alex, you really shouldn't do those types of tricks."

SEVEN

Tigger's birthday cards stop at the same time I understand the truth about the tooth fairy, Santa and the Easter Bunny. It is the year of the 'Killer Kid' skateboard.

Dylan Brindle works at the same surfboard factory as Dad – DB Surfboards. He is good friends with Vili's family. Dad's latest interest is making the two-part moulds to shape plywood layers into skateboard decks. He gifts Dylan three decks, so Dylan will custom-spray a fourth for my birthday. No shop boards have custom sprays. Mine is the first. It has a clawed monster, part alien and part robot, and two words – Killer Kid. I love that board so much it's like an injury every time the paintwork scratches. The spray is on the underside so every time I put the board down at the back to do an ollie it's jump, hop, *scrrr-aatch*.

At the weekends, I go to the netball courts in the school grounds. The open-air corridors and steps outside the class-rooms are sick to jump off. Some of the older kids bring poles and ramps. I've only had it a couple of weeks when an older kid comes up to me. He is a bit like my pal Chris – plump with no muscles. "That's a sick-looking board, dude. Give us a go." I want to say, "No, sorry. It's special to me. I've only had it a few weeks," but I don't want to sound like a little kid. "Okay, but no ollie kick-flips."

He pops the board, kicks it, does a three-sixty and lands back on the board. *Snap!*

He hands it back. "Sorry kid, these things happen," and he walks off. You can't trust older kids to do the right thing because they just care about themselves. It's not all the kid's fault. My dad used cheap plywood. It's cheaper than the plywood used for boats, but it's not as strong and flexible.

The whole walk home is a watery blur. Broken-hearted, it is my first real loss. I swear only ever to have cheap, plain boards after that. I feel sad for many months, until the day Dad and I visit two of the guys from his work, Brent and Archie. They are eighteen.

Brent is the sprayer – his dreadlocks are awesome. He and Archie are best friends and live near the lake. Archie's mum has allowed him to turn the whole house and the backyard into a skatepark with wooden ramps. It has a soft magic that skateparks don't have with their sound of hard plastic wheels on concrete. Archie's moves on ply are noisy but cool – a low, smooth-rolling, running whoosh.

Archie takes us into his shed in the garden. I look up at the ceiling. There, nailed, is every board he has ever owned. *All snapped.* It isn't like a graveyard in the sky where broken boards go to die. It's incredible like a museum. All the halves have made Archie a better skater. I get it. Learn from your stuff-ups, no need to feel sad. When I'm back home, I take my board from under my bed and put it on the top shelf of my bookcase.

My dad knows the people from work but has no friends. Not like mum. Mum tells me it's because his big family just keep to themselves. His father died when he was fifteen – he was an engineer. The family lived in Pymble, which is over an hour by train from where he went to school at Bellevue Hill, so Dad never played with kids from his school. He was on a scholarship. That's why it confuses me when he does things that make no sense like the skateboards, and when he never locks his car when we go for a surf, has stuff taken and still doesn't lock it.

I am a first-rate skater because really, they are just a surf-board for land with wheels instead of fins, and I'm a natural on a surfboard. They're better than a video game because you create the puzzle. When I try new moves, I discover I must be patient and respectful with my board, or we'll both end up broken.

I prefer the school ground and Brookvale's small industrial estates. They are more real and challenging than the moulded parks. I can't tell you the feeling I get when I do a humongous drop, land it, and wait for three minutes. Here it comes … adrenalin. The rapids.

TEN

It's three years since the visit to Archie's place. I'm learning that shattered and heartbroken doesn't just apply to objects.

It applies to families too. Dad left two Christmases ago. I was on the verandah when I heard them fight. I had the feeling something was going to happen and, when it did, they took Nattie and me out on the verandah to tell us they were separating.

I'm between a rock and a hard place. My solution? Keep active. If I'm all body and action, I'm not uncomfortable feelings I can't handle. What sort of dad leaves just before Christmas? Mine, apparently. Dad wanted to come back three months later, but Mum said no. We're officially a family that's lost a corner. We're triangular now – me, my six-year-old sister, Nattie, and Mum. I don't like losing things, and I don't like change. Surfing and skating are my lifelines. But it's tough to realise what you love now feels lonely. It's like the difference between being in an empty house and being in a house when someone else is at home but in another room. No more Dad in the morning. No more Dad after school. No more Dad every weekend.

Mum reckons in the UK 999 is the number for urgent assistance. In Australia it's 000. Mum has triple zero money. Mum never seems to panic. She just gets on with things.

She has a great sense of humour but now, most of the time, it's hidden behind the look of a person on a mission. One thing I *am* sure of, no task is impossible for Mum. Almost immediately after Dad leaves, she takes in Japanese students – boys and girls. She treats them like family and sends them cards at Christmas when they are back home. We all learn some Japanese, help them with their English, take them on outings. Our house feels fuller, more like home.

After a year, when Nattie is settled in school, Mum begins work as a cleaner even though she used to be a teacher. She always drops us off at school, picks us up and likes it if we come home dirty 'cos she knows we've had a kid's sort of a day. Mum says thanks to Napisan, no mother can complain. I say, "I'm taking that that is some sort of prescription drug or alcoholic drink."

"Very funny, Alex. It's a laundry soaker for the sort of kickarse stains some kids bring home."

Mum still makes killer lunchboxes with notes in them. *Have a great day. Love you. Suggestions welcome.* We have no family in Australia, and Mum doesn't want us to be latchkey kids. Grandma died when I was two and Grandpa when I was six. My aunt and uncle live in the UK. Dad's mum treats us more like guests than family. Dad's brother has no interest in being an uncle. He is a live-at-home-with-mum hermit. All he does is work. My dad's family never deal with things. You can't talk about something serious, state an opinion or invite discussion. They are like those jellyfish, innocuous blubbers, who try not to be at the mercy of wind and current, preferring to drift passively. Dad's life, and the life of his immediate family, is black and white and grey.

At least 2000 is an awesome year at school. 5C. Mister Capewell. Brilliant. All the kids love him. He is strict but funny and fair. Mr C makes everything interesting. Convection: energy equals action. How did he show us heat results in movement? No chalk and talk with Mr C. There we all are, in pairs, with a square of aluminium foil, a teabag and a pair of scissors. Mr C is savvy enough to hold onto the cigarette lighter till needed.

"Don't we get cups, hot water, milk and choc chip cookies with that, Mister Capewell?" The other kids laugh. I get called Choc Chip by Mr C for the rest of the lesson. Fair enough. We cut off the ends of the teabag and empty all the leaves, leaving us with a cylinder of fine paper.

"Put the cylinder *vertically* on the foil. Elijah, that's horizontal. I've always suspected you're vertically challenged, which is why you're our best soccer player, and a danger to yourself and others when it comes to climbing trees," Mr C says with a firm softness. The whole class laughs.

That's another thing I like about Mr C, he never blames and shames. He's respectful. He can somehow point out a mistake and have you feeling good about yourself afterwards. I suppose it's that he wants the best for every student in his class.

"We're all a family in this classroom," is his spoken mantra. I wish he were my dad. My dad never actually tells me he likes me. He just makes wisecracks.

"Okay, Choc Chip. Light the way."

Mr C hands me the lighter. He doesn't need to tell me what to do. It's obvious the tube needs lighting along the top edge. I'm sure most of us are thinking, *What the hell, we all know paper burns.* Then, as the flames burn most of the way down, the cylinder suddenly flies upwards. *Holy cow! A flying teabag.* It's the best way to understand how a hot air balloon works. It lifts off the ground because the air inside is less dense, and therefore lighter, than the cold air outside. Then Eli, always one for a good story, calls out, "Any good stories about hot air balloons, Mister Capewell?" Mr C ignores his question. Eli immediately shoots up his hand. Eli doesn't mean to disobey the rules. It's just that his body runs ahead of his brain.

"Aha, Elijah, I know what you are going to ask, and I shall respond. I do have one, but it is not *my* story. Hands up who wants to hear the Lawn Chair Larry story?"

All twenty-six hands shoot up.

"Larry Walters's boyhood dream, since he was thirteen, was to fly. Poor of sight, he could not be a pilot in the US Airforce. So, this is what he does. At the age of thirty-three, he takes his Sears aluminium lawn chair and forty-five helium-filled weather balloons, a C/B radio, a sandwich, beer and a camera. For stability he weights his chair down with water bottles and tilts the seat back forty degrees. He puts on his parachute and belts himself into the chair."

I can't help myself. I stick my hand up.

"Don't tell me you need a toilet break, Choc Chip?"

"No, Mister Capewell. I just want to ask if you know why Americans don't eat snail sandwiches?"

"Because they're not French?"

"No, because they only like fast food." Everyone groans, then there's complete silence. All eyes and ears are on Mr C.

"Oh, I forgot to mention he also has a pellet pistol. Why do you think that is?"

"To shoot something," Eli shouts out confidently after putting up his hand and receiving a go-ahead nod.

"Spot on, Elijah. But what?"

"Anything that flies, like pigeons, crows, geese, eagles, ducks."

"That's quite a list, Elijah."

I shoot my hand up.

"Yes, Alex."

"I think he doesn't want to shoot what flies but what floats, the balloons. He will need to land the chair eventually, so he must let the air out of the balloons."

"Well, the classroom's two greatest minds have solved the mystery. Well done, boys."

Mr C continues, "When his friends cut the cord, which anchors the chair to his Jeep, Larry does not float up slowly as expected; he streaks into the sky as if shot from a cannon. A hundred feet ... a thousand feet ... sixteen-thousand feet. He levels. He's at the very high altitude of Mount Everest Base Camp – temperature roughly minus 16.7 centigrade. He cannot risk shooting his balloons. He drifts for more than fourteen hours. Close to freezing, he decides to risk shooting some of the balloons."

The ultimate showman, Mr C pauses and scans the room. We all know there is a question coming. We must earn and learn the rest of the story.

"Would it matter which ones he shoots at first? ... Yes, Sarah."

"If Larry shoots them all at once he'll come falling too fast, and if he shoots them all on one side he'll be unbalanced."

"Spot on, Sarah. He shoots them in a balanced manner. However, he has not planned on accidentally dropping his pellet gun overboard. The remaining full balloons slow his descent, and he tangles in power lines on the way down."

I am sure we all have a look of horrified dismay on our faces. The whole classroom is an, "Oooh, nooo!"

"Relax. Unharmed, Larry Lawnchair dangles 1.5 metres from the ground and causes a twenty-minute electricity blackout for which he incurs a fine."

The recess bell rings. We always wait, even the antsy ones like Eli and me, till Mr C dismisses us – row one, chairs in, out you go, and so on. Today he reminds us, "Don't let me get any calls from your parents telling me you've spent all your pocket money on helium balloons from the party store *and* borrowed your grandpa's deckchair. Neither will cut the thirty-three cubic feet of helium in each of Larry's balloons. Party store balloons are only five cubic feet of helium. That's one hundred and forty-one grams – the weight of three Curly Wurlys. A single helium balloon is only useful to those wishing to sound like Daffy Duck. Class dismissed."

I already have two great ideas for the cost of one balloon, three of my favourite chewy sweets and my spud gun. A third idea comes to me. Nattie will be amazeballs by the flying teabag. From another of his hands-on lessons, I learnt a lot about air pressure, all from a wooden ruler, a piece of paper and a karate chop. I remember because I provided the ruler ... *Snap.*

Sometimes I am a shit older brother. I don't play much with Nattie now because I am out with my friends. I think I would be better at brothering if I had an older brother. Just this week I was sitting on the couch playing Super Mario on my Nintendo 64 when Nattie came up to me.

"Alex, can I sit next to you and watch?"

"Okay."

If I defeat Bowser on this level, I get another key to the third floor, kick his ass for good and rescue the princess. Mario grabs Bowser's tail and swings it round and round to gain speed. Boom. It hits one of the bombs. I'm almost there. I've defeated Bowser twice, but I've used all my coins to bring Mario to life again. This is it! No mistakes. When Bowser jumps, he produces shock waves. *Jump, Mario, jump!* But I'm not quick enough. I am so mad I turn on Nattie. "It's all your fault. You should have stayed quiet."

It's a lie. It was my mistake, not hers. I need someone to blame. See what I mean about being a shit brother? When I'm frustrated I get verbal and physical. I push her as far to the other side of the couch as I can, pushing my foot against her stomach. I push so hard she's pressed hard against the padded arm of the sofa. She farts. I'm lucky Nattie had baked beans and not eggs for breakfast. The sound fills the room. She must have top-notch muscles in her sphincter. Thankfully, it's not that disgusting bad egg smell that's hydrogen sulfide. As it wasn't foul-smelling and really toxic, I'd rate it as the passing of pure wind. We don't laugh. I want to say, "I'm sorry", but the words stick confused between my head and my mouth. My chest's superglued and I feel hot – my heart's shrivelled and black like it's disowned me. I feel so bad I just want it to go away. Instead, it's Nattie who goes away, and I am alone. I focus on my game again 'cos it's the best way to make the bad feelings go away.

It's Mr C who taught me, scientifically, fart is an acronym for Frequency Actuated Rectal Tremor. If you cut out Mr C's heart and held it up for everyone to see, you'd announce,

"Behold, the heart of the best teacher ever." He'd act as a warning to those crap teachers out there like the one who has a year four class. I'm sure the kids curl their toes up in his class. His nickname is Beetroot. I think he should join FART – Federal Association for Retired Teachers. That's where a 'Furious Anally Rejected Turdair' belongs. I reckon you shouldn't be teaching if you can't control a class of eight to nine-year-olds without volcanic activity. Actually, in the free dictionary online, fart has twenty acronyms. Most are to do with fathers, farmers or firemen. Fathers Against Radical Teenagers, Fast Action Response Team, Fathers Against Rude Television. I have one to add – Father's Absent, Really Traumatised.

After school I feel lost, so I go down to The Point at Dee Why Beach on my own to surf. Sometimes, I also go at five in the morning before school. I love surfing. It's so fast and easy. Some kids' mums hassle them about surfing – *Do your homework first*. Mum never does. She understands I need to wash the seated school day out of me more than I need to knuckle down to homework at four o'clock. Good on you, Mum. Just wish I had an older brother as a surfing buddy. At weekends Dad and I surf. He never tells me what he thinks of me. Mum says he is proud of me and thinks I'm a competent kid with sound judgement who is loyal and friendly. I wish he'd say that to me.

Today I surf with Dad at Marquise, which is the middle section of Narrabeen Beach. I am forever on the scorch of anger lately. All I want is the surf to chill me out. I take one look at the ocean. It's crap, but I'm desperate to catch a wave.

Anger rises like a surging thermal spring. The conditions are choppy and paddling out is hard work. Wave after wave, no sets worth take-off.

I walk out of the surf in a foul temper dragging my board after me with the leg rope still attached. I pull it across the beach backwards with the fins dragging in the sand – I'm feeding the fury. Crap surf. Hot ice fury. I'm coming up to the wooden planks on the sandy slope leading up to the grassy area. Sitting like railway tracks, they don't accommodate a surfboard dragged backwards over them. I'm ropable now.

Fuck.

Fuck!

Fuck!

I stumble and sprawl. I feel like a prick – humiliated by my anger. I've let it take over at any cost. I can see Dad is trying not to laugh. He never fucking takes anything seriously. He takes the board off me. We sit in silence on the way home. I don't even thank him for the lift.

THIRTEEN

We don't have weekend on, weekend off with Mum and Dad. Mum lets us visit Dad whenever we want and vice versa. Nattie goes more than me because I have lots of friends to play with on the street. Kids on the street – they're like magnets. It doesn't take us long to find each other.

Cam lives across the road from me, but we don't go to the same school. He and I don't intend to get up to mischief, but usually our curiosity leads us there. Mum says her fondest memories as a kid growing up in the sixties were the adventures she got up to with her friends. They would be out most of the day and come home for dinner. She says it does a kid good to be free away from the adult world, to explore and get up to minor mischief. If I make a mistake Mum never lectures me, instead she always says, 'Alex, would you like to hear a story?' She knows I am going to say yes. Everyone's a sucker for a story. Mum's cautionary tales are often about things she did as a kid that she shouldn't have. Sometimes she will share something more recent, which is what happened when she had to pull me up about a lie, but I won't go into that now. I've a better story for you – the time Cam and I came back to my house with a look of heated triumph. I think Mum didn't tell us off then, or tell a story, because she knew we learnt our lesson about an aerosol can and a lit match. She was right.

It began as a perfect autumn day that ended up in flames.

Cam's not a real active kid. He prefers to play computer games. His parents think I am hyperactive, but Mum thinks he is underactive. His parents smoke and never take him and his sister anywhere. I don't think he's ever been the other side of the Harbour Bridge. If they hadn't lived on the Northern Beaches, I doubt he would have seen an ocean ever, much less swum in one.

Down behind his place is a massive tract of natural bush and a section of concrete tube big enough to crawl in. The tube is waist-high, tipped at a slight angle and chock-a-block with spider webs. Probably funnel-webs. But that proves to be the least of our worries. We decide to blast the spiders, and the closest weapon we have is Cam's aerosol deodorant. Or maybe it was WD40. I forget. We spray the webs till we hear the faint asthmatic wheeze of the can. Then, Cam has one of his not-so-brilliant ideas – a box of matches. Immediately I know this isn't going to be good. I step back. Cam looks into the tube and throws in a lit match. What I wasn't expecting was an explosion.

An entire funnel of flame shoots up with the sound of the exhaust on an old bomb of a car. It engulfs Cam's whole head. *Fuck! Shit!* I feel the colour drain from my face and scalp. I'm imagining images of melted, raw flesh and Cam's head, mummified under white bandages, healing to gnarled skin. *Please don't let that happen.*

Cam is so lucky – frizzled fringe and eyebrows, with the look of someone with a sunburn in desperate need of Aloe vera. He was never agile and quick-thinking like me. I reckon too much food and not enough exercise makes you slow.

The end of year six comes around fast. Cam is not on the street anymore. His parents, like Vili's, are renters. I bring the yearbook home, *Off to the Future*, where our class have written about dreams and plans. Mum reads mine and the others. "Oh, my goodness, what questionable values some of these parents instill in their kid's dreams: 'good job that earns good money; find a job with large paying salary and do something good like skydiving; hope to be wealthy; ten years from now, be a famous tennis player or accountant for the NRMA and own a boat and private jet.' Whatever happened to letting twelve-year-olds be in the moment?"

I've almost finished my first year at Narrabeen High – only six weeks to go. It's a Wednesday and, true to the child's rhyme, I end up a child of woe. A six o'clock sunrise surf ends not with a wave of crimson anger this time but with a piece of paper.

> Mona Vale Hospital Discharge Summary V 022-57-09
>
> Date of Admission 13/11/02
>
> Final Diagnosis: Lacerated R foot
>
> R foot – large flap. Tendon on view dorsum lateral R foot.
>
> Significance in Investigation: X-ray – no fractures
>
> Neovascularity intact.
>
> Operation: Debridement and washout lacerated R foot to suturing with Applicate backs lab.

It's a normal morning at Dee Why Point. Plenty of waves rolling in, and plenty of people rolling up. I've already caught a wave and come in towards shore. I'm close to the whitewash, with more sets rolling in. Paddling to the left is my best bet to miss the impact zone of the waves. I duck-dive two, and then paddle out on the diagonal as fast as I can to get out wide. I get to the face of the last wave of the set and duck dive again, but each duck dive is like two steps forward and one step back. I've another five minutes of hard paddling if I want to be carried back less. On my third dive I've almost made it out of the wave when I see there's an older guy on a seven-footer already riding the wave. He goes out of his way to cut close to me even though he's more manoeuvrable than me. He's after the best hit of the wave. He's one of *those* surfers – all competition and no etiquette. As the swell lifts me I try to paddle out of his way but as I pull out of the wave, my feet still underwater, there's a sound like two pieces of two-by-four lumber hitting together. Then, sharp pain and numbness. As my feet come up I bend both my knees with my feet skyward – his fin has sliced my right foot like a switchblade.

The entire outer side of my right foot, from above the toe to below the ankle, is a flathead that's been filleted by a fisherman – it flaps back and forth, barely attached. I yell at him, *"You fucking shit. FUCK. You fuckwit. Look what you've done!"* The water swirls with blood, and the salt water and force of the waves are Vlad the Impaler. I scream like a stuck pig. The guy pulls me to the beach.

Buggy.

Lifesaver tower.

Ambulance.

Mona Vale emergency for four hours.

Wet suit cut off.

Expensive accident.

By the time they're ready to clean out the sand, Mum is there. *"Oh my God,* you look like a wounded soldier." Her face is all anguish and concern. That's the thing about my mum, her face, like her words, have no subtext. What she's feeling and thinking is always written as clear as day on her face. Horrified and shaken by the size of the slice, she's still together enough to challenge their choice of a local anaesthetic. She insists they put me under.

When I see Dad that weekend, all he says is, "It was an accident waiting to happen. You need to pull your feet in."

Feet take a long time to heal. Can be problematic. Four days later I'm back in emergency. There's an infection in the wound, so they open it up, wash it out again and re-stitch it. I stick to skating till it's fully healed – no water till the stiches are out. It's over two months before I surf again, but I've learnt a hellacious lesson: duck dive, don't dangle.

If I try, try, try new skate tricks I turn off thinking, and my body and brain are in the present, free of regret and fear. When I skate I am the space between the simplicity of instability and the complexities of flat ground. Forwards, backwards, spinning. Board – face down, face up, face out. The best? The weightless moment when I am no longer going up or down and I have time to manipulate the board, collect it and land.

Centrifugal force.

Inertia.

Connection to ground, motion and texture.

Speed is king.

I never walked if I could ride. Now, I don't walk if I can skate. My body feels like a motor that is continuously running.

Nattie's nine now. Mum says she's as smart and independent as I am. Well, not quite. She's more a cuddle person than I am.

Although Mum is flat-out, she still makes our lunches. Opening my lunchbox is like opening a present or putting my hand in a lucky dip – all my friends wish they had *my* lunchbox. Every compartment has something different in it, and no two days are ever the same. The contents are always healthy but do include a small, less healthy treat. Mum says a bit of sugar is suitable for kids like me 'cos we use up so much energy. Small apples. My mum knows kids have more important things to do at lunchtime than eat through a gigantic apple, plus she hates waste. I ask her one day, "Mum, where'd you get all those different treats from?"

"Oh, here and there."

Then I work it out.

Her cleaning takes her to the city and back. That's a lot of small supermarkets, corner stores, Japanese and Asian marts. Sometimes she buys the Japanese lemonade in the glass bottle with a metal clip and a glass marble in the bottle. The first time I have one I trick Eli. I open it, take a swig, and then hold it above his head.

"Alex, what the hell do you think you're doing?" He waits for the fizzy downpour, but the marble blocks the neck of the bottle. "That is *sooo* cool. Can I have it?" He's my best friend, and he's a trickster like me. He doesn't have to ask twice.

We stayed on in the house when Dad left. Where we live is the centre of my universe. It's like the middle of a compass: north to Narrabeen Lake, south to Warringah Mall, east to Dee Why Point and west to Red Hill's bush and trail bike tracks. What more could a kid want? Perhaps for his parents to still be together.

I'll never forget the day Dad left us. I do miss us being a family. I'm still thinking … come back with us and start over again. But if someone were to ask me, "Do you think that's likely to happen?" I'd bite my bottom lip and avert my eyes upward till I'm in control. "No, not at all."

FIFTEEN

My son has a need for speed. His first motorbike is an ex-postie bike – sixty cc. He is not impressed with its twenty k on the flat and only slightly more impressed with the sixty k on the downhill. He is a boy on a mission to own a Yamaha 170xz. He works out it'll cost him one thousand and fifty dollars he does not have. He has a plan. He speaks to his dad who informs me, "Alex is at the age where there is work he can do in the factory, and he is mature enough to want to do it." Alex heads off every weekend working for a pay rate that any kid working at McDonald's would die for – fifty dollars for two to three hours work. One weekend when Rob comes around to pick up Nattie, I ask, "How's Alex going with the work?"

"We work well together, as it's a two-man job. Alex enjoys it. He gets a lift there and back with me. It's the best lead a young guy could have into work."

"So … what's he doing?"

"Well, he helps with pouring the blanks. I weigh out the chemicals, mix them and, while I'm doing that, Alex ensures the mould is ready for the pour by taking out the previous blank and removing the paper liner. I do the pour and close the mould. Then we do it all over again. I also get him to clean out buckets in which I mix the foam. I have a single-phase motor–"

"Whoa, that's enough, Rob. You lost me at 'single phase motor'. Thank you for all that. Good to know our son is a hard worker."

Rob and I have an amicable split and, apart from the odd minor spats (usually over money), we are civil to one another. Neither of us is the sort of person to use our children as point-scoring darts.

I pop into the factory one weekend when Alex is working. It's like walking into a vigorously shaken snow globe whose contents refuse to settle dormant on the floor and, instead, cling in relaxed defiance on the horizontal and the vertical alike. Alex's face is as white as an Antarctic explorer. He stops the blower. Another of his jobs – to collect the debris and bag it.

"Glad to see you're wearing a mask."

"Dad gives me the mask he uses. It stinks because he always has tuna for lunch."

I say nothing but have a quiet word with Rob later.

After three months, Alex has five hundred and fifty dollars. Rob matches it. It's after that, Alex meets Jamie and the two become friends. Jamie's parents pick up Alex and his Yamaha to take him and Jamie to Mini Wheels at Ingleside. By sixteen, Alex has outgrown Ingleside and his bike because there are so few places he can ride it without needing a lift: Pacific Park is an hour and a half away in the direction of Wiseman's Ferry and Dural.

Mid-adolescence, and some of his teachers regard him as troublesome. I suspect he's smoking marijuana, but I never smell it on him, and I am not going to search his room. I remember my mother, when I was fifteen, opening a letter a boy wrote to me. All very innocent. She did it when I was an adult too. Always suspicious. I won't break my son's trust. What's the saying? Trust takes years to build, seconds to break and forever to repair. Sometimes never repaired as was the case with my mother. I'll have to find the right moment to chat with Alex.

It is hard for him without a male to influence him and act as a mentor – all the influences are mine. The male teachers at high school range from the adored to the loathed. Adolescents don't tread lightly. They rage, rage against the incompetent, the inconsistent and the petty. Alex had a passion for science from primary school but, now he's at high school, it's been chalked out of him. "What's happened, Alex?"

"It's that dickasaurus, Mister Frack!"

"I'll ignore the swearing for now. I'm assuming you mean he's a poor teacher, and his methods deserve to have died alongside the dinosaurs."

"You got it, Mum. He either dictates straight from the science textbook, adding a few of his own words or expects us to copy from the chalkboard. He writes so much he has to wipe-out what's already on the board to write the rest. It's impossible to study from my incomplete confusing notes and, when I explain this to him, do you know what that screw-up's answer is? 'You're slow. Write quicker.' He has no idea how difficult it is to look up, look down, remember what to write, write while trying to spell the difficult words, then look back up, trying to find where on the board you were, to write the next bit. Even the kids who finish have no idea what they've written."

"Why doesn't he just give you a handout? Have you highlight the topic of each paragraph and then the supporting ideas?"

"Because he's lazy. Too much trouble to organise himself and make sure he prints the sheets for the lesson. Besides, if he did that he'd have to actually teach. I end up frustrated and feeling less-than, so I play up and he sends me out of the class for the entire lesson."

"The whole lesson?"

"Yup, and he's done it before."

I ring the school and organise a meeting with the school principal and the teacher. Alex comes with me. "I am concerned about Alex's removal from the classroom for entire lessons. It's not best practice to banish a student from a class for such an extended period."

"If he behaved himself it wouldn't happen," is his teacher's response.

I certainly will not let him get away with that; let him take bloody responsibility for his inferior teaching methods. "Perhaps if your lessons were not predominantly chalk-and-talk and dictation, and you made accommodations for a student with difficulties associated with both, you would not facilitate poor behaviour." Outed, he blushes a deep scarlet. The principal is in a difficult situation; the teacher and the school cannot appear to lose face.

"Look, I think Mister Frack's teaching style may not be a good fit for Alex. I can see his science report from primary is exceptional. How about we move him to Science A. It's the top class."

I let them save face because all I care about is my son's well-being.

Two weeks later I ask him, "How's the new teacher?"

"He's got long hair and acne scars, but he's a great teacher. Dad is working with me on one of his projects."

"And …?" Sometimes it is like wringing water from a dry rag trying to get information out of a teenage boy.

"Oh, yeah. It's making a car out of a mousetrap."

Something is shifting. I need to listen more than I talk. When I pick Alex up from school, with a friend in tow, is the time their backseat banter fills me in on his life.

Once he would have said, "Mum, thanks for going to school and sorting things out," or, "Look what Dad and I have made."

Once …

EIGHTEEN

My son changes school to the newly opened Senior Campus in Brookvale; it only takes years eleven and twelve. A lot of kids prefer it because it is a more mature learning environment. There he comes across another Mister Frack but this time in woodwork and metalwork, a subject he finished top of in year ten at Narrabeen. Alex looked up to that year ten teacher in the same way he'd revered Mr C. A poor teacher can destroy a kid's passion, and then comes disinterest and falling grades. "Don't tell me he's another Frack, Alex?"

"Pretty much. He wouldn't know how to hit a snail on the head with a hammer never mind a nail. He's hopeless. He dislikes it when I question him when what he's saying doesn't make sense. He picks on me."

"Picks on you? Give me an example."

"We had to make three joints. Anyway, I thought mine were pretty good. He gave me five out of ten for each joint and told me to fix them. I went away, fixed them and went up to him again. He marked each one with a different score than before, but the overall rating was still fifteen out of thirty. There was another boy he liked, and he gave him twenty-six out of thirty. I think to myself, *That's bullshit. Mine are way better.* I borrow the boy's three joints and take them up to the teacher as if they're mine. 'Here. They're fixed.' He says, 'You've made them worse.' He scores them less than my first ones and says, 'Go away and do them again.' You know what I took away from that lesson? Men with power can be petty and vindictive. They should be mentors to boys, but they try to suck who you are right out of you with their meanness."

Increasingly, I am aware there is an anger brewing that is more than the turbulence of adolescence. Does Alex feel let down by his father? An intelligent man who can build anything but who, shielded from the world by a wounded over-zealous mother, is incompetent in the ways of the world. Is it the incident with Albirt? A boy thinking, what idiot gives half the business to a stranger?

Rob sets up his own surfboard business in a small factory in Brookvale's industrial area. He makes all the moulds the resin is poured into to form the blanks for the surfboards he then custom-shapes. Always looking to improve the formula, Rob takes on Albirt, a Lebanese guy who is a chemist, or so he says. Rob knows him as the sales rep for a chemical company DB Surfboards use.

Mistake number one: Rob gives Albirt half-shares in his fledgling company based solely on Albirt's assurance he can improve the formula. Albirt's claims turn out to have the integrity of the selling techniques of a used car salesman intent on offloading a lemon. It takes only a few months for Rob to realise that Albirt knows as much about a winning formula as some Chinese companies do about safe and nutritious infant formula.

Mistake number two: Rob flys out to Mexico to help an American businessman set up a factory from scratch: make the machinery, train the workers. The job is a four-month stint. I advise him, as gently as I can, he is running a considerable risk leaving the country with the set-up as it is. Albirt can't be trusted. Rob leaves Australia for Mexico without dissolving the company and, upon his return, discovers Albirt has paid no rent, and Rob's six-thousand-dollar bond on the factory is null and void. He also returns to an empty factory. Albirt has stripped it of all the machinery. Within weeks, it is clear Albirt has also run up debts in the company's name and, as co-owner, Rob is fifty per cent liable.

Apart from the one teacher, there are two other incidents I have to sort out when Alex is eighteen and doing his motor mechanic apprenticeship. He's completing a T3, which means he does a day at TAFE, a day training in the workforce and three days at school on his HSC.

The first incident involves laziness, and the second lie and bluff; both reflect poorly on the police. All I can say to my son is, "They're jaded and bent and only interested in breaking the broken. They're like sports stars that misbehave: completely blind to the fact that they have a responsibility to be role models for those younger than them."

I grieve that there is no strong loving male in his life, including his father, who can say, "You've got a beautiful, strong heart, and I'll show it to you in action through my actions. You're a sensational young man, and I know you're better than three-quarters of the way there to being a man. Any troubles we'll sort out together." My son desperately needs a mentor to draw him in inch by inch, to applaud his growing ability to analyse and spot incongruities and pettiness in others. To help him understand and integrate the negative modelling of others without losing trust and hope. Thank god he's had a few male teachers who have modelled that. Sometimes all a boy needs is one person who gives him a sense of what it is to be a good man.

The first incident occurs when Alex is on his learners. We're in my Toyota taking it steady down Howard Avenue towards Dee Why Beach, Elijah in the back. As we near the cafes on both corners, the driver in front of us suddenly starts reversing at speed. I can only think he's passed a parking spot and decided to backtrack without checking who is behind. He hits us.

It's a narrow, busy road and it's a problematic spot to stop, but there's no choice. The driver, a male in his late thirties, storms towards us, leaving his car door open. "Why don't you do a better job of supervising. Your son just ran into me."

"There's no need to be aggressive. You backed into us." I point to the one parking spot that is behind us, "You obviously–"

"Just shut up. I did not *obviously* anything. Like to see you prove I backed into you."

Elijah, standing close to the man, whispers to me, "I think you should call the police. His breath smells of alcohol."

I call the police, but it takes them an hour and a half to arrive. During that time, Elijah and Alex cross the road to speak to the café owner. They return with a look of a successful reconnaissance mission. Of the two people eating outside the café, one is the owner; he's seen the whole thing and is willing to give a witness statement.

As soon as the police arrive, the man's manner changes. Suddenly, he's Mister Nice Guy after being so rude, misogynistic and aggressive to me. They take a breath test. He's over 0.05. Why they bother asking him when he had his last drink, I do not know. "I've had three drinks over the past three hours, officer." He's a smarmy veteran who knows how to suck up to the police, and he knows his reading is already one and a half drinks down by the time they arrived. It will be down by the same when they test him again at the station. Despite telling the police we have a witness, they decide Alex is to blame simply because he was at the rear. They book him. Alex is to lose his Ls, have a reckless driving charge on his record and a five hundred dollar fine.

I ring the police first thing in the morning the next day. "Has the driver been charged?"

"No, there were no charges."

I'm furious knowing I can't do anything about their decision; however, I can about something else. Late in the afternoon, I visit the café owner, obtain a witness statement and find a sympathetic, young female lawyer who agrees to a flat fee of five hundred dollars. She says it is lazy policing – a common occurrence. Before it reaches court, the police withdraw the charges.

When Alex is about to turn eighteen, his dad takes him out along the used car strip of Parramatta Road. He will only lend Alex two and a half thousand. Alex chooses a VL Commodore with a rear-wheel drive. Why rear-wheel drive? For all the wrong reasons that are the right reasons for a teenager – drifts and burnouts.

I take Alex to pick it up. Mount Druitt – a place of the vanishing Australian Dream. I don't think I've ever been to the suburbs west of Sydney. It is an area of social exclusion, unemployment and addiction. I never see the man who sells it to him, but Alex says he's sure he is Arabic, not Pakistani. While we're waiting, a car speeds by playing loud hip-hop with explicit lyrics. You might have to look out for yourself here, but I bet people also look out for one another here too.

Alex rings the owner on his mobile; he'll be there in twenty minutes. I take one look at the car. It is an eighteen-year-old's wet dream. A striking custom spray over the bonnet of a semi-clad, *Penthouse*-style, snake woman – all boobs, a ribs-removed waist and long flowing hair. I don't want to burst his bubble. I say nothing other than my admiration for the quality of the artwork. I am sure my ex-husband warned him. I am sure he put up no resistance to an insistent son who wanted a car to drive his mates around on the weekend. Sure, he didn't offer to lend Alex just a little more money to steer him toward something as enticing but more appropriate. The naked truth is, I know this car will be trouble.

The second incident with the police is just before his eighteenth birthday. On a Friday night Alex gives a lift to two boys and their backpacks at the end of an alcohol-free party in Forestville. He detours to the shopping centre to use an ATM. On Saturday morning there's a call from the police station in Dee Why. Alex is to come in for questioning. He doesn't refuse, and I go along as his support person.

The policeman interviewing seems wet behind the ears; he's undoubtedly in his early twenties. The offence is 'marking public property'. Alex's car number plate has been identified on CCTV footage and linked to unknown youths seen spraying graffiti.

"What are their names?"

"I only gave them a lift. I don't know who those guys were or their names."

The policeman looks put out. Does he think Alex is lying to protect friends? He changes tack. "Why were you parked at the shopping centre?"

"I needed to get money out of the ATM. I've got the receipt if you need to see it. I left the two of them in the car, so I've no idea what they did while I was getting the money. They were in the car when I came back."

"You were seen on the CCTV footage spraying."

"I couldn't have been because I didn't do it. I just went to the ATM."

Then it's as clear as day to me. The CCTV footage of the incident is blurred. The police officer has lied. He wants to lay charges at my son's cost. Appalled, I step in. "I believe my son when he says he wasn't involved. I'd like to see the CCTV footage." He hasn't expected this.

"It's not readily available. We'll wrap it up for now. If we need any more information, I'll be in touch."

I turn my head and body away from him as my mouth, throat and stomach fill with acidy revulsion. Bluff and lie to obtain a conviction? Would he have pulled this trick on a young man with two parents present? On a young man not dressed in trackies and runners? I doubt it. I am too full of the thick black goo of moral disgust to be angry.

We never hear from him again.

It's Sunday, early afternoon, and I'm exhausted. Single parenting. Work demands. Money worries. An angry adolescent for whom I am not enough.

Solid ground around Alex and me is opening like an earthquake. The smooth land, once so easy to traverse in any direction, is now fragmented – dislocated into chasms and incoherent islands. I am losing him.

Only a couple of hours before I transmute into mother mode when the children return from a sleepover with friends. I need to grab a pick-me-up nap before I nip to Coles to top-up on bread, milk and a few staples. Sleep, a cocoon away from all the daily demands. Blessed oblivion. I lie down and immediately fall quiet and deep.

I dream.

My subconscious freewheels. Moments from the movie of my mothering.

The little boy with blue, buckled sandals and snowy hair who rests full against me, his arms around me.

The boy with his legs akimbo on the toilet, his face belight with a cheeky grin.

The boy at the sink with a smile, rubber gloves up to his armpits and a sink full of bubble-bathed dishes.

The day my son ... how old would he have been? Maybe six ... didn't want to hold my hand. Didn't like the look of the tortuous, blue rivulets under my skin. It hurt, but I understood. For a child it is a matter of fact statement without prejudice. It carries no intentional hurt. I'm no fan of my hands either.

The edge of my fatigue gone, but still drowsy, I turn and look at the clock. I wish I could lay here longer, but I've only forty minutes in which to do the shopping. I rinse my face and my thoughts with cold water, finger-brush my hair, grab the car keys and leave.

Now, it's not images but thoughts that tumble and stray like the contents in a clothes dryer without the non-crease, delicate cycle and end button functions. Now, it's not my son's childhood years. It's his wildhood years. I know that what happens during his adolescence will shape his destiny. I do not want him to be a broken boy, an incomplete man.

To discipline an angry male teen is nigh impossible for a single mum. I'm trying to salt and pepper guide him, sparingly, but it's like trying to wrestle a giant octopus and expecting a favourable outcome. I understand how my best intentions to support him are unconsciously castrating for him. It is not the natural animal order. He despises me as I try to balance on a tightrope of nurturing and limit-setting. What my son craves is an experienced male to mentor him and help him self-regulate his anger. It pains me that I cannot provide this. There is no village to support him in the wilderness.

He will have to form the man he is from fragments.

As I drive back from the supermarket I do some deep breathing. I'm only just put the shopping away when I hear the front door slam. Alex comes in to the kitchen without saying hello and goes straight to the fridge for a bottle of Solo.

"Hello, Al. Good to see you. How'd your weekend go?" As he turns I realise, somehow, I've made a mistake. I can see the angry fever in his face, the intent to wound.

He moves up close and incredibly loud to deliver his ugly, desperate words.

"You're a bitch! A loser!"

My insides collapse like a failed souffle, but I stay calm and measured. Underneath the fire I know his words are purely water and air . "I may be many things, but one thing I know I am not, is a bitch. No one has ever called me that."

He says nothing, turns, hightails it up the stairs and slams the door to his bedroom.

I do not know why he thinks I'm a loser. I have provided stability. Perhaps it's the lack of money, and maybe it's that I am still single without the male in his life he desperately needs.

I will never forget that day. Sunday. 16th March 2008.

The day he squirted those words like ink from an octopus. Both of us hidden in the dark cloud of it for weeks.

Aiden died yesterday.

I was the last one he called – eight-thirty p.m. on a Saturday night.

"Hi, mate. How ya doin'?" His voice was a little slowed and slurred. He was slightly pissed. "We're heading to Mona Vale Hotel. Wanna come?"

"Sorry, Den. I'm really knackered. Had a big one last night."

"Come on. You know you want to."

I say I will. "See ya there." But I fall back to sleep.

He was dead by eleven-thirty.

The morning after, fifty of his friends, including students that were in his year, meet at Boondah Park's legal graffiti wall in Warriewood to paint their tributes. It is the one time I know the police to do the decent thing and look beyond their badges and notebooks. They ignore the under-age drinking because they can see all the boys are distraught and inconsolable. When I return home in the afternoon, drained and distressed, I lose it with Mum, although I never told her why. I call her a loser and a bitch.

Within four days, he's eulogised, burned and buried. I am too cut-up to go to the funeral. I don't want to believe he is no longer here, that I'll never hear his voice or feel his hand collide with mine on a high five. That I'll never …

I spend days curled up in my bed, my legs to my chest, bawling into my pillow. It is the dragging that horrifies me the most. Without that, maybe Aiden would have stood a chance.

Weeks later I wonder if I'd been there, even pissed, if it would have made a difference. I see myself walking with him, close enough and quick enough to push or pull him out of the way. It makes me so fucking angry when I read the suggestion he was playing chicken. He was one of those guys that never drank and drove. He didn't live on the edge. He didn't need to prove himself. He was always happy, and he had a loving family with a mum and dad. Maybe that was the secret of why he was who he was.

Aiden and I would go driving together and just hang out. We got along well. We'd both finished at Freshwater Senior Campus the previous year and entered the motor trade as apprentices – me a mechanic, he a spray painter. We were both loyal, hard-working employees.

Even his best mate Harry, who knew him since he was six, said if you were his friend he treated you like a brother. He was loyal too. One time when he and I visited some of his mates, I was drunk. I'm a loud, happy drunk. His friends fully bagged me out. "Den, why are you hanging out with that dipshit? He's pissed."

"Don't talk about him like that." He turned to me. "Let's go."

We left with me sober enough to appreciate what he had done. I wish now I'd said what I was thinking: "Cheers, bro. You're a legend."

The loss of Aiden was hard on everyone, especially his family and Harry. Aiden would have gone far. He had that sort of personality and work ethic.

Mona Vale is one of the worst suburbs on the Northern Beaches for drink-driving offences. Barrenjoey Road near Kitchener Park has six lanes. Keeping drink-drivers off the roads needs to include pissed pedestrians too. He was lagging and stumbled and fell as he reached the middle of the northbound lane. A State Transit bus with passengers didn't just hit him, it dragged him ten metres.

Now, my obsession is no longer watching every episode of the make-believe antics of the West family in New Zealand's drama-crime-comedy series *Outrageous Fortune*. Who gives a shit about understanding families when you can be alive one day and dead the next? Why care, when your life becomes death, police stations and unhappy families? Now, my obsession *is* scrolling through *MyDeathSpace.com* looking for entries for male, eighteen-year-olds.

Troy. Found dead almost three years after he went missing.

Paul. Died in a single-vehicle wreck.

Ryan. Struck and killed by lightning.

Nicholas. Swept to death while watching a sunrise.

Phil. Killed in a motorcycle accident when a car turned into his path.

The list doesn't include those who deliberately set out to harm themselves.

I throw caution to the wind with everything I do. I become pure instinct. No rules. My dope-smoking worsens, but at least it helps me forget, helps me to sleep deep and dreamless. It relieves the pain by taking the edge off the nightmares of living. I have 'Carpe Diem' tattooed on my body. I do a burnout in my car in front of the police station and all sorts of other minor shit.

For my birthday in June I ask everyone to give me money. I collect five hundred and fifty dollars. I go back to Bill's Custom Tattoos, the studio in the city that did the Polish eagle on my ribcage when I was seventeen – a tribute to family and heritage. I've no idea why I chose that part at the time. It's the most painful part to tattoo on. All bone and no flesh, and I'm six foot three and lean. This time I leave with five tattoos: a tribute to Aiden, a court jester, a dice, a skull and the words, 'To Each Thier Own'. Mum nicknames the fifth tattoo, 'Two Dyslexics in a Tattoo Parlour' but later retracts it, as she can see the misspelling is ironically apt.

I'm also still trying to cope with the terror that overwhelms me that began with Dad's reaction to Albirt's betrayal – his mute acceptance rather than rage. I'm continually trying to evade intolerable sensations: the churn in the pit of my stomach; the tightness in my chest; a heart in overdrive; a parched mouth; hairs standing up on my clammy skin. I'm at sea, alone, without a compass, no mariner to teach me how to navigate by the stars.

Dope is the only thing that calms me. Exhausted from a surf, my body will keep pushing me beyond the exhaustion because, inside, I feel like a motor that won't turn off. I've read that experts say kids with undiagnosed ADHD self-medicate with dope. Dope also dumbs down my gnawing hypervigilance to the cost of not becoming a mature man. My father is powerless to reassure and guide me. I've come to realise it's my responsibility alone to piece together the puzzle – I'm not going to see the revelation on a bumper sticker. I've lost all respect for the police. Mum was wrong on one thing – respect. With my generation it's not a given – you earn it. Also, there are only so many times you can suck the soul out of something before it goes pear-shaped, beyond repair.

My fears spew forth as anger. I become oppositional, defensive and reactive as I look desperately outward into the world to find out what it is to be a good man. I mainly witness what it is not. I'm forced to mortise-and-tenon joint my manhood from antonyms. Lost and bewildered, I begin to blame Mum when things go wrong. It's Nattie on the sofa all over again. I punch holes in my bedroom walls. After the second hole, Mum says calmly, "Alex, this can't go on. You'll have to sell your Nintendo and your games." I take it on the chin. I pack up my Nintendo and thirteen games for Cash Converters, along with my Hot Traxxx racing cars. I get the seventy dollars to fix the wall. Am I angry with Mum? No. I'm pissed at Cash Converters. They've ripped me off at two dollars fifty for a fifty dollar game. I vow never to go there again.

I'm super-colossal volcanic activity waiting to explode like Mount Tambora in Indonesia. I'm a country without borders. Mum is trying to contain me, but nothing is working. Nattie shrinks into silent withdrawal. I am unable to place limits on myself. The whole house is stressed, not just the walls in my bedroom. Mum's face is gaunt and pale. Although I'm eighteen I have another year of school, and Dad has cut the maintenance. The day my dad tells Mum I overhear, "Rob, I'd like you to reconsider. He still has another year of school."

"He's eighteen. Legally, I don't have to pay towards his upkeep anymore."

Mum's not a bitter person. She's tried. She accepts the situation. Money's tight as she's taken time off from work to do a month's fulltime refresher course with the Department of Education so she can teach in Australia. She's waited till

Nattie is settled in high school, and till we are both more independent and can safely get to and from school ourselves. There are no permanent positions, so she's a casual. She keeps on a private cleaning job for three hours on a Sunday, in Kirribilli, for a retired couple.

I am a mother in a war zone. Nothing is changing. Nothing's working. We are lost. Lost on a sea of hot ice in a boat without lifejackets. Up till now, Alex has enough control not to hit me, but this time he's particularly enraged and, I can see in his eyes, gritted teeth and up-close, raised fist, he's tottering. He smelts against the confusion of trying to work out who he is. I run inside the house and lock him out. He's on the roof; he's seen the open main bedroom window. The race is on. Barely there before him, I close the window and swivel the latch. He's swearing and shouting. Next thing I know the police arrive. Am I okay? Do I want to take out an Apprehended Violence Order? On my son, who's floundering around like a speared fish? That is not an option. I have to put an end to the hurricane games. I now know why cyclones have people's names.

Constantly frustrated and bewildered, Alex regresses to infant-like tantrums with the verbal and physical power of an adolescent – more holes in his bedroom wall, verbal confrontations. The vortex he has become (arguments, aggression, disrespect and disparagement) requires containment. I need to shield Nattie from it as well as myself.

I give him an ultimatum. Either control your anger or you can't move with us to the new house.

It's a move I knew we'd have to make once Nattie settled into high school. I can't keep the mortgage on my own, and I've done my dash maintaining a weatherboard home with pressed metal ceilings. I didn't realise I was demanding the impossible of Alex. I may as well have said, "You can't live with us anymore." Instead, I thought I was offering him a choice.

I am not entirely sure I am exiling him to a safe place to figure himself out. Rob steps up to the responsibility of housing him. Alex moves in to Rob's mother's garage for a few months, but it's a long cycle ride to where he works. The home of three, now two, has an emptiness that hangs in the air like an unfinished sentence. He will have to cut and paste himself into a collage of what a man should be.

How I need someone to reassure me with, "Do not worry, your son will come back. He will have learnt humility, and he will not be broken by it." I rely solely on gut-instinct and wise counsel from two of my closest friends, Mike and Jeni. I place trust in the past, in the relationship I once had with my son and the qualities of self-sufficiency he had as a child.

I check with Rob how Alex is doing. It's not always reassuring as Rob is utterly unable to sense mood and emotion.

I don't hear from Alex for six months until the day he turns up distressed and overwhelmed. He sits on the unforgiving hardness of the concrete kerb, his feet in the gutter, his back curled, his hands cupping his head. A primal howl like a maimed wolf tears the air.

Startled crows on overhead wires scatter into the shattered silence and swirl screeching into a pale, anxious sky. I feel the umbilical cord of my son's distress. It is more than the previous dramatic emotional outbursts of the past, unlike the one I witnessed in the hall before he moved out when I caught him turning his head to glance at how he looked as he offloaded.

At the time his outburst shocked me. Was he checking out how impressive he looked? It registered as outburst, press pause, replay outburst. After that, I never took his emotional outbursts as serious signals of deep distress. All tornadoes blow in and blow out when Dorothy thinks she wants to be somewhere else other than home. But *this* one it is more than that, it's raw and instinctive. It's full of hopelessness, humiliation and fear. Tenderness wells up in every cavity in my body, and all I want is his desperation to breed courage, not recklessness. I must trust that the stability of his early childhood will stand him in good stead and that what he has within him is strong enough to weather the challenges imposed by the outside world. I have faith in both. However, today as he sits in the gutter, I wonder if it will be the last time I see him. *Please, please … don't let it be the last time.* I tell him if it's all too tough he is welcome home.

"No. I don't want to come home. I want to make my way myself." He wants to return when he's figured things out. When he's able to look back at something he didn't figure out and can say, "Ah, that's what that was about."

He pulls himself together. As I watch him leave, a gossamer tremor of sadness rises in my chest, then to my throat and silent tears weep down my cheeks. I am grateful that Nattie is not home.

Parents make tough-love decisions in the hope their child will grow up. The hitch is that not every child is gifted with resilience or the skills to overcome adversity and challenge. The call comes.

Attempted suicide fighting for his life.

Death by suicide.

Drug overdose.

Car crash.

Please God, do not let it be *my* child. Boundaries have nothing to do with loving a child conditionally. They are a genuine, and loving, attempt to steer a child.

TWENTY

I'm back home. My room in the new house is a replica of the old. Everything in it is as my room was eighteen months ago – my bed, my bookcase with the broken skateboard, the box of assorted skateboard parts under the bed and the non-favourite t-shirts I left behind in the built-in robe. All that's different is an orange envelope on the pillow and a box of Cadbury's Favourites. I slowly peel back the envelope flap and take out the card: *Welcome home, son. I love you. Always have, always will, Mum xxoo.* I take a deep breath and windscreen-wiper my hands across my eyes. My chest is an unsettling swell of regret and shame.

Disappointment and anger were all locked together inside me then. Hissy fits like a lit match in a box of fireworks: swearing, screaming and punching holes in the wall. I knew I had to stop that shit, but I couldn't – the anger always took over. I think about the day Mum asked the impossible of me and cast me out into the real world. Mum did the best job she could. I well up thinking about what happened. I regret her seeing her son like that. There's the saying, 'You fuck it, you fix it.' That's what I am doing now – putting all my energy into the sort of person I want to be. I don't want to be pigeonholed in my yesterdays.

There's nothing like a bit of hardship and adversity to make you grow up. It was tough walking away from home on an apprentice's wages. I was earning two hundred and fifty a week, and my rent was a hundred and fifty dollars. I was paying off a State Debt Recovery of fifty dollars a week because I wanted to clear it as quick as I could. After bus fares, it left fifty dollars for food and extras. To save on bus fares I cycled from Long Reef to Avalon Garage. In good traffic, an hour each way. There were days I didn't have much to eat. I'd eat lunch and skip dinner unless it was wedges or two-minute noodles.

An empty wallet and an empty stomach taught me humility. I realised how hard it must have been for Mum. She wasn't a loser. She was kind of heart, fierce of mind and strong of spirit, and I've discovered I've got more in me than I thought – like mother, like son. By the third year of my apprenticeship I earnt five hundred dollars a week. That eased things up a bit for me.

Friends ... I was so fucking lucky to have Nate and Danny. In trouble, we'd be there for one another in a click of a finger. We were like brothers. With Nate we'd fight over something but he was able to overlook it and move on. Combine that with honesty and a great sense of humour, and what more can you want in a friend?

Dogs … I've brought one home with me. Monty. He's a cross between a boxer and a German shepherd. For the size of his body, his legs are skinny. The guys I shared the house with said I was a natural with him.

After I've finished putting my stuff away in my bedroom, I glance out of the window onto the decking below. Monty's dozing on the sun lounge, his back-leg twitching. I go down to him. I rub my hands together until I feel the heat between them, then I bring them together just enough to sense the energetic connection without allowing them to touch. I let them hover above Monty till I feel a tingle in my palms and fingers. Gently, I place pressure on him – on and off, on and off – till his uppermost back leg relaxes and drops. It's what I call loving him to death. Whenever I'm feeling down he makes me feel better. He relaxes me. I start to cut back on the dope.

I feel proud of Monty. He's couch-surfed more than I have, but he's so well-trained. Mum thinks he is a real gentleman. I can take him for a walk in the bush, stop to pee behind a tree and return to see him waiting patiently for me even though there is another dog off-leash nearby.

I remember how it went down when I first looked after him for this lady who was a friend of Casey's mum. Casey lived in the share house with me at Avalon. She left Monty with me for a few months. The woman returned, said money was short and could I look after him. Said, if I didn't take him, she'd have to give him away or take him to the pound. I couldn't let that happen 'cos I know if no one wants them they move them between pounds for awhile and then put them down.

The share house at Avalon was dilapidated. The owner was renovating it while we lived in it. He was a mean bastard. He tried to steal my boat's motor by hiding it in his garage. "I'd like my motor back, mate."

"What motor?"

"The one that's in your fucking shed."

He also tried to fleece me of my bond because Monty bit his dog. Monty was tied up and just lying there. Monty was so obedient. If I was crossing the road he'd sit at the edge of the path and wait. He wouldn't move till I called him. Anyway, the owner's terrier is off the lead, running repeatedly between the back and front of the house following the owner. It decides to steal Monty's bone and tries to run off with it. When it came to food, Monty sure had firm boundaries. When the ranger sees how docile and well-trained Monty is, he shakes his head and tells the owner it's his responsibility to keep his dog on a leash.

Mum writes about Monty after I'd had him for two years. The poem is still in the box with his ashes. I can only ever read it to line eleven before my eyes rim with water like a glass about to overflow, my chest constricts, and I feel the urge to run in the dark, dank night till sweat douses me. Run, run, and keep on running until my brain follows my body into exhaustion and oblivion.

He died.
We cried.

It rained –
a gentle patter in the darkened September night.
Drained by tears and warm memories, we remember
– his undemanding, well-mannered nature
– the sashaying of his hips and tail when he was excited
– his spontaneous, appreciative licks
– the bones and chicken wings he loved as treats.
Now, he lays in his tent, his back towards me.
I pat his coat wishing for some magic that would breathe a
rise and fall into his ribs.
Sweet, sweet dog.
The sky cries and thunders for your loss, you creature of
the heart.
The grass will grow back where you've yellowed it.
The flower beds will fill and blossom anew.
The sun will still warm the lawn where you lay.
But …
The scene will never be as full as it was with your presence.
We loved you, Monty, and we will remember you always.

That lady, the last owner, told me she had taken Monty to the vet because he had a small benign growth in his hip. I suspect she knew it was cancerous. *Shame on her!*

THIRTY

The mother and her two children are sharing a Christmas. She is now sixty-six, and they are twenty-six and thirty. The mother has never wanted the three of them to be a family where the awkward and essential are left unsaid. "When you didn't move with us all those years ago it was the most heart-wrenching decision I've ever made. I did not do it lightly. It was the only call I could make as nothing else succeeded in changing things. When your anger made you punch holes in the plasterboard walls, I suggested a punching bag and cushions, but you wanted to see your anger manifest as damage. This gaping hole into the void and blackness, its jagged, fragmented edges, *this* is my anger. From the day you left, any teenage boy I saw in the street was not a stranger. They were *you*."

"You're right about the holes. After a while, bottling everything up was like what happens to the contents of a Coke can when you shake it and pull off the tab. I acted like an idiot the day you locked me out, and I climbed on the roof. I've quietened down in ways. I've learnt to handle my frustration. I know how to say, when I'm agitated, 'Let's talk about this later.' Only five simple words, but it's a genius technique."

"Have you forgiven me for how tough that transition was for you?"

What the mother hears next from her son's lips creates only one thought. *If I were to die now, I would die a happy woman.*

The son says, as their eyes meet, "It was the making of me."

Her eyes tear up and her full heart outpours with the simplicity of, "I'm so proud of you. I love you."

"Thanks, Mum. I love you too. Hand me your iPhone."

"Why?"

"Because it doesn't feel like I'm truly home for Christmas until I've taken your phone and said, 'Here, let me show you,' at least five times."

They both laugh.

She has her son again.

Alina Loneck was born in Nottingham in the UK in 1953 and has lived in Australia since 1976. She has an Honours Degree in Psychology and English Literature from Leeds University and a Bachelor of Visual Arts from Sydney College of the Arts. Whilst she has written and published non-fiction, this collection is her first publication of fiction. Although an educator and artist, her most precious roles in life have been as mother and friend.

Also, by Alina Loneck

Non-Fiction

Opals, Rivers of Illusions, Gemcraft Publications.
Index ISBN 978-0-9092232-4-3

Fiction

Love is a Many Splendored Things, Cilento Publishing.
ISBN: 978-0-6450004-3-6
A collection of forty-seven short stories due for release in mid-January 2021.

My Thanks and Acknowledgements

My heartfelt thanks to my two beta readers who gave me feedback from a reader's point of view. Helen Lambert, dear friend and kindred spirit, your input, dedication to the task and unwavering support made all the difference. You're my ideal reader, as you have the wisdom of a sixty-year old with the free spirit of a twenty-six-year-old. Chris Carter, another dear friend, I thank you for providing a male perspective and for acting as a sounding board for the contents of 'Losing Una' – a story close to home for you. To anyone reading this and thinking, '*Oh my god, she's friends with a bestselling author*'. He's not *that* Chris Carter. However, he is the first edition by a decade.

My joyous thanks to the illustrator Sandra Wood who is friend, artist and alchemist. I so enjoyed collaborating with you. Your pen and inks bring the essence of each story to life.

To my precious, long-term friend Jennifer McAleer. You are always there through sunshine, shadow and dappled shade. Always generous with your time, clarity of thought, enthusiasm and constant loving support.

My acknowledgement and thanks to the developmental editor Helen Williams who assessed my pre-final draft. You pinpointed the strengths in my writing: psychological precision, ability for drama but also nuance, the courage to get down and dirty with the hard truths and to amuse and offer insight.

We are not always fully aware of our talents and strengths till someone points them out. Thank you for that, Helen.

My deep gratitude to Evan Shapiro of Green Avenue Design and Cilento Publishing for the stunning cover that perfectly mirrors the content of *Within Sunshine & Shadow* as well as the style of my writing and that of the pen and inks. Always patient, personable, knowledgeable and generous with your time, you're designer, advisor and part wizard. I trusted my book in your hands from the very start. Your level of care was exceptional.

Finally, an acknowledgement to my two adult children, Alexander and Natalia. You are both my most precious, creative contributions to life. You are my blood and indelible ink. I love you till the last drop and last full stop.